Praise for Noelle Mack

THREE

"A truly sensual story that will titillate and captivate readers."
  —*Romantic Times* (four-star review)

"Smoldering hot, naughty adventure . . . a deliciously kinky read."
  —*Joyfully Reviewed*

"The queen of seduction meets the king of rakes. Sensual, sexual, stupendous. THREE is a fabulous erotica romance."
  —*Harriet Klausner Reviews*

SEXY BEAST (with Kate Douglas, Noelle Mack, and Vivi Anna)

"Quite entertaining . . . and the heat rating is off-the-chart hot!"
  —*Romantic Times*

"Noelle Mack's *Tiger, Tiger* is a sexy romp . . . charming and funny . . . and steamy."
  —*Romance Reviews Today* on SEXY BEAST

Red Velvet

NOELLE MACK

APHRODISIA

KENSINGTON BOOKS

http://www.kensingtonbooks.com

Aphrodisia Books are published by

Kensington Publishing Corp.
850 Third Avenue
New York, NY 10022

ISBN: 0-7582-1390-5

First Trade Paperback Printing: September 2006

10 9 8 7 6 5 4 3 2 1

Printed in the United States of America

for JWR, with a wink

Contents

The Knockout

1

Sofia picked up the remote and turned off the baseball game with one press of her press-on fingernail. The screen went black. "They lost, Ruthie. Pay up," she said with a smirk.

"How could they do this to me?" Ruth wailed. "I love the Mets."

"Then you're a fool for love. You owe me."

"Guess so." Ruth grabbed her beat-up purse off the coffee table. She took her wallet out, parted the leather folds, held it upside down and shook out a bus ticket. "But I'm broke." She shook the wallet again. A small blue feather drifted down.

"Is that all you have?" Her cousin raised a perfectly tweezed eyebrow. "A parakeet feather and a bus ticket? I shoulda known."

"That's right. Until next Friday." Ruth mentally calculated the budgetary impact of losing a $50 bet to her cousin. "You know this means no new birdcage for Bambino. No new raincoat for Tuff." Her little mutt looked up at Ruth with a sad expression, and jumped on the couch beside her.

"You're breaking my heart." Sofia tapped a cigarette out of the pack in her other hand and sucked it between her lips.

"No smoking."

Sofia gave her an insulted look and spoke around the unlit cigarette. "I'm not smoking it, I'm sucking it. Do you see a lighter in my hand?"

"No. Just wanted to make sure."

"I don't smoke unless I see an ashtray, and this is your place, so no ashtrays. Okay, tell you what. I'll give you the cash."

"Huh?"

"The Pet Palace on Fordham Road is having a sale on bird-cages," Sofia said in a coaxing tone. "Beeyootiful white wire bird-cages with bonus plastic bell. The Bambino would love one. But if you take the fifty, you must do my bidding. You said you would."

Ruth groaned. "Oh yeah. That contingency clause I suppos-edly agreed to—you mentioned it at a critical point in the last inning. I don't remember anything except the outfielder drop-ping a fly ball."

"I do."

"So tell me. What do I have to do?"

Her cousin looked her up and down. "Get dressed up and get out in public."

"No."

"You can't say no. You want that fifty, I know you do. All you hafta do is strut your stuff and that ugly dog in front of Mrs. Agnelli and all the neighbors and God himself." Sofia took the cigarette out of her mouth and crossed herself with it in her hand. "Who will not believe that you actually own nice clothes."

"I don't. You gotta lend me some."

"Not a problem." Sofia cast a disparaging glance at Ruth's sweatpants, grubby T-shirt and scuffed sneakers.

Tuff made a yarping noise. Ruth pulled the dog closer to her. "He's upset. You didn't have to say he was ugly."

"I was being polite," Sofia pointed out. "And it won't kill

you to get dressed up and get out. All you do is sit in this rent-controlled apartment and write those freaky little poems. You haven't worked in, what, a year?"

Ruth shrugged and stroked Tuff's coarse fur. "I'm on hiatus."

"Yeah, from life."

"My dad told me to find myself before he died. You know he left me money. Not much, but enough."

Sofia took the cigarette out of her mouth and eyed her narrowly. "At least that whore he left your mother for five years ago didn't get it all."

"No, because Mom had a good lawyer. And she's been living it up ever since at Lake Como," Ruth pointed out.

Her cousin shook her head sadly. "Which means you have no one to look after you but me. I'm tellin' ya, Ruthie, their divorce gave you a complex. You think being happy is wrong. You didn't even have a good time in college. No, you hadda go and major in English, so you could be unsuccessful. You don't go out, you don't date. And you need a makeover anyway."

"Thanks a lot." Ruth glared at Sofia, who set down the cigarette and took out a compact. Parting her lips, Sofia examined her long, sweeping eyelashes for glumps of mascara. Not a glump in sight. Ruth wondered how Sofia managed to look so good just to watch a ball game. "For your information," she began, "I have been thinking of writing experimental short fiction instead."

"Oh, please."

"I have a few chapters of a novel on my hard drive. Does that impress you?"

Sofia shot her a hopeful look. "Is it a romance novel?"

"No. But the screenplay I started has romantic elements."

"You could write for the soaps!" Sofia's expression was awestruck. She even looked at Ruth instead of the little mirror in her hand.

Ruth only shrugged. Her cousin was a lifelong fan of *The Young and the Restless*, a show that Ruth privately thought of as *The Hung and the Reckless*. All the characters did was sleep around with everyone in the little town of . . . what was it called . . . Glandview?

She snapped out of it when Sofia clicked the mirror shut and gave her a worried look.

Ruth sighed. Her cousin meant well. "Okay, okay. When it gets dark, I will put on borrowed finery and go for a walk." Tuff wriggled with enthusiasm and yarped loudly. "Uh-oh. He heard the W word."

Sofia stuck the cigarette back in her mouth and frowned, making it hang down. "Why dontcha get a normal dog? He can't even bark."

"Later, Tuff. Not now. When my evil cousin goes home. She's making this up anyway. I never agreed to this."

Sofia shook her head. "Where's my handbag?"

"What does it look like?" Ruth said innocently.

"Black patent leather mock croc. As if you didn't know. You're stalling for time."

"Why would I do that?"

"Because you're afraid I kept the proof." Sofia lifted her coat and found the handbag. She scrabbled through it, then thrust out a crumpled piece of paper.

"That's your handwriting," Ruth said indignantly. "And your words."

"You signed it."

"Five months ago."

"A bet is a bet." Sofia smoothed out the piece of paper and read aloud. "I, Ruth Caterina Pirelli, biggest idiot in the five boroughs, swear to pay my beloved cousin Sofia $50 next time the stupid Mets lose, because I think they can't lose. And I have to do whatever she says if I can't pay."

Ruth hugged her dog. "Kill her, Tuff Stuff. Eat the bet. Save me."

Sofia got up and put on her coat, still talking around the unlit cigarette. "I'm gonna drive home so I can smoke this thing and see what's in my closet. Then I'm coming back. Before the sun goes down."

Unaccustomed as she was to pantyhose and cold to the bone, Ruth flipped the finger at Sofia, watching from inside her car. "You planning to drive around after me?" Ruth asked.

Sofia rolled down the window. "Nah. I gotta get back in a few minutes. Lou's making carbonara sauce. He always screws it up unless I hover."

"So you trust me not to skitter right back through my door, huh? Tuff, quit yanking me around!" The dog stopped pulling and gave her a who-me look, then lifted a leg and did his business on a hydrant. At least he was happy. And Bambino would be happy in a new, bigger cage. Ruth was not happy but she could always write a poem about it. She tugged down the black leather micromini her cousin had picked out and turned up the collar of the matching, tightly fitted black leather jacket. The top underneath was buttoned all the way up but it wasn't going to keep her warm.

"Did I say I trusted you? Walk." Sofia pointed a fingernail. "To the end of the next block. While I watch."

Ruth walked. The red velvet high heels Sofia had insisted she wear had half-inch platform soles, which made her sway, then stumble, with every step. The dog, pulling hard on his leash, didn't help.

She swallowed a mouthful of hair, then dragged it out of her mouth. The spring breeze was whipping her long, dark hair around. Between it and the wraparound sunglasses she'd insisted on to conceal her identity, Ruth felt like a blind person.

With the world's smallest Seeing Eye dog. Who was doing his best to drag her in front of the bus coming down the center of Hughes Street. The red velvet high heels were killing her.

But her humiliation was not complete. In the brick house next door, Mrs. Agnelli came to the picture window under the two-tone metal awning, clutching a dustcloth for the figurines she kept on the sill. Her eyes widened when she saw Ruth.

Ruth turned around just long enough to see Sofia wave good-bye from the car at the corner. She heard her cousin take off and held her head high, shortening Tuff's leash so she could walk quickly by the house. She wasn't fast enough to escape the notice of Mr. Agnelli, who rustled up out of the camellia bush he was pruning in the small front yard and stared too.

She picked up the pace, dragging Tuff for a change. This *was* a walk. He *had* peed. The sparse grass of early spring that edged the sidewalks couldn't be that thrilling, not even to a sniffing fanatic like him. But once she got around the corner, he planted his paws and refused to budge. Oh, yeah—one of the natural wonders of her Bronx neighborhood, the World's Most Fascinating Hedge, was just ahead. She'd meant to go the other way but the Agnellis had distracted her.

Tuff loved that hedge, had to sniff every leaf and then lick it, the little perv. And then he had to sniff the World's Second Most Fascinating Hedge down the next block.

The hell with that. Sofia had driven away, and Ruth was going to get around the corner and through the alley to the back of her apartment building. Just why her cousin thought this experience would be good for her, Ruth didn't know.

She looked down at Tuff, then up, and did a doubletake. A white stretch limo with tinted black windows was careening toward her. On the sidewalk. She grabbed her dog, pressed herself into the scratchy hedge, and prayed. The stretch limo came to a stop about a foot away. She let out her breath.

The guy at the wheel rolled down the back window and then

popped the trunk, stabbing at unseen buttons until he got the passenger side window down. He leaned over to it and yelled at her. "Hey, Gina! Hop in!"

"That's not my name," she snapped.

He seemed taken aback. "Ain't you Gina? They said she'd be on this street, maybe walking her dog."

Friggin' idiot. All the same, she softened her tone. "What a coincidence." She didn't want to argue with someone who was so stupid or so drunk that he drove a limo on the sidewalk. Ruth wasn't even sure she wanted to step out of the hedge. The dry twigs prickled her but she stayed where she was, clutching Tuff. "Lots of people have dogs," she added, hoping he would go away.

He didn't. The limo door swung open and the driver got out. "Ya sure ya ain't her? I'm s'posed to bring Gina to Brooklyn. You know, for dinner with *la famiglia*." He leered at her.

Tuff growled. Ruth wasn't sure if her dog had ever seen a real, live goombah but he was seeing one now. The man wore a sagging, badly made black suit that pulled across his beefy shoulders and a black sweater underneath it. Ruth glanced down. Yeah, his pants were creased to kill, but too short for his thick legs. And he had on narrow, custom-made loafers that pouched out around his bunions.

"Why're ya in the hedge?" he asked curiously.

"I didn't want to get run over and I was afraid you didn't see me."

The goombah laughed loudly. "No, no, I saw ya. All of ya. That itsy-bitsy skirt don't leave nothin' to the imagination. I was drivin' on the sidewalk for laughs because I thought ya were Gina. Ya live around here?"

Ruth emerged from the hedge and set Tuff down. "No. Gotta go. Nice talking to you."

"Hey, wait a min—" He shut up when an unmarked police car pulled up next to the limo. The car was a gleaming navy blue and it looked brand new. Maybe a hybrid. Neither of them had heard it driving down the street.

She looked behind the wheel, hoping it was a cop she knew. Actually, it was driven by a detective she knew, although the tinted windows made it a little hard to see him. At least she thought Nicky Del Bianco had made detective. He was super-smart, a John Jay graduate with a master's in criminal justice who'd started out as a beat cop just because he wanted to, in the Bronx neighborhood they'd all grown up in.

And he was a total sex god. Always had been—some of the younger nuns even used to check him out on the sly in high school. Nick was unbelievably hot-looking, with dark-gold hair and tawny skin and olive green eyes with thick black lashes. From northern Italy—well, his father was. Maybe a little Swiss in the genetic mix, maybe Austrian? Ruth would have to ask Sofia, who prided herself on knowing things like that. His mother was from the south, Calabria, like practically everybody else in this neighborhood, Ruth was pretty sure.

Her cousin still got stars in her eyes when she talked about Nick now and then, even though she'd been married forfrigginever to Joey Castiglia, who was almost as hot. But no one was as hot as Nicky.

Ruth looked through the windshield at him. He was resting his large, strong, tawny hands over the steering wheel like they were lion paws. Able to break the neck of a goombah with a single blow.

Stop thinking like Sofia, she told herself sternly. Ahead of her by a few years, her cousin had gone through Catholic school with Nicky, writing SOFIA + NICKY♥♥4EVER and **Sofia Del Bianco (Mrs.)** and the names she wanted for their children—Nicky Jr., Anthony Marco, and Brianna—on the inside covers of her notebooks. Hoping to get somewhere, somehow, with him, Sofia had even attended mass when his mother did, Nicky being conspicuously absent from Our Lady of Mount Carmel on most Sundays because he stayed out so late on Saturday nights. But as far as Ruth knew, Nicky had never even kissed her cousin.

The other man looked at him uneasily as Nicky got out and kept the car between himself and the two of them, leaning on its roof. He took a small ID folder out of his jacket pocket and flashed his shield in a bored way. The high-gloss paint reflected his killer smile upside down as a killer frown. Ruth had a feeling he knew the goombah and didn't like him. "Ignazio. Long time no see. Who's your friend?"

Huh. Nicky didn't recognize her. Ruth was about to open her mouth and enlighten him when she realized she would be enlightening the goombah at the same time. She clammed up.

Ignazio gave a theatrical shrug. "We just met."

"Uh-huh." He looked directly at Ruth. "Is he bothering you? Need a ride somewhere?"

"Okay." She picked up Tuff again and edged past the limo driver, who was sweating.

"Get this boat off the sidewalk, Ig. Don't make me run the plates. I don't even wanna know where you stole it from."

"I didn't steal it," the limo driver said, looking outraged.

Nicky shook his head as if he didn't want to hear another word. The sunlight hit his dark-gold hair just right, Ruth noticed, and the breeze ruffled it. Even though he was standing on the other side of his car, he was tall enough for her to see through the window that he was in plainclothes. As in faded jeans. And a nice shirt that the breeze kept pushing against his body. Chest to die for, biceps ditto. He'd been a golden boy in high school and he was a golden man now.

It crossed her mind that maybe Sofia had set this up—but no, that couldn't be. Ruth had gotten incredibly lucky, that was all.

She wobbled to the unmarked car on those goddamned red velvet platforms. Safe in her arms, Tuff indulged in a few parting growls at the goombah.

"Go back to Brooklyn, Ig," Nick said quietly. "Don't let me catch you around this neighborhood again."

The other man opened his mouth to protest, then shut it again. He got behind the wheel of the limo, puffing a little, and slammed the door. Then the same fandango with the windows started again—up, down, up—until he figured it out and drove very carefully off the sidewalk, maneuvering the white limo with a little more skill than he'd shown before.

Nicky watched him go around the corner and turned to her. "Where to? I'm Nick Del Bianco, by the way. Detective NYPD."

"Um, that way," Ruth began, gesturing vaguely. He really didn't know who she was. Interesting. Very interesting. She decided to change her destination and go someplace else besides home. "But could you drop me on 187th Street instead, near Arthur Avenue? At De Lillo's? I want to get a cannoli." She did want one—the crunchy sweet tubes of pastry filled with flavored whipped cream were her favorite treat.

He looked at her like *she* was a cannoli, grinning like a hungry wolf. "Sure."

Like mirror images, they opened their respective doors, got in and closed them at the same time.

"How about that. Simultaneous . . . never mind." He grinned at her and started the car. Tuff wriggled so he could look out the window and then he yarped. "Is that how he barks?"

"Yeah, when he's happy. Thanks for rescuing me. I mean, that guy wasn't really bothering me, but I was kinda nervous."

Nick drove, keeping his eyes on the street. "They don't call him Ig the Pig for nothing." He didn't say anything more for a minute, just went left and then right, moving into the center lane.

"Oh, so you, like, know him?"

"He's on our list, put it that way. Why was he talking to you? I could tell you didn't want him to."

"The fabulous Del Bianco, psychic. How'd you pick that up?"

The fabulous Nick looked at her and gave her a half smile. "Just observant."

"He thought I was someone else. Someone named Gina, who was supposed to go to a thing in Brooklyn with *la famiglia*."

"Got it. Gina Bertelli. She works the motels near LaGuardia now. You do kinda resemble her, at least in shades and that outfit." He gave her an appreciative glance. "But you're a class act all the way and she—uh, she isn't. Believe me, you don't want to spend a sun-filled, fun-filled weekend with that *famiglia*." Nick slowed down and a gypsy cab behind him honked. He waved the guy around. "Hard to find a spot near De Lillo's."

She looked ahead on the bustling street, thinking fondly that the neighborhood had hadn't changed much. Her mother's falling-apart photo album from her 1950s childhood showed the same brick apartment buildings with Art Deco details, butted up against much older tenements. And the people hadn't changed much, either.

The local women still shopped almost every day, buying everything fresh, going in and out of the stores: Borgatti's for pasta, Calandra's for cheese, Biancardi's for meat, Tino's Salumeria for cold cuts, and Randazzo's Sons for fish. They sniffed and sampled everything, gossiped, prepared to stock up shelves and refrigerators that were already crowded with good things to eat. Ruth pointed. "Up ahead."

Nick pulled over into an empty spot by a fire hydrant. "Okay. You and Tuff enjoy yourselves. I'd stay for a cannoli, but I gotta get back to the precinct. See you around, Ruth."

She pulled down her sunglasses and looked at him with mingled disappointment and amusement. "You knew it was me all along."

"Yeah, I remember you tagging around after your cousin Sofia. But you were always so shy. Pretty, though."

Ruth gaped at him. Had Nicky Del Bianco really thought of her as pretty? The thought was mind-boggling.

"But you had me fooled for a little while. I really didn't recognize you at first. So are you in disguise or what?"

"Kinda. I lost a bet on the Mets."

Nicky gave her a pitying look. "They never win any more."

"Sofia made me pay up by dressing me like this."

He gave her a long onceover. "Yeah? She did you a favor. You're a knockout in that. Can I have your number?"

Ruth swallowed hard. She wanted to scream it to the heavens—*Nick Del Bianco wants to hook up with me!*—or at least into Sofia's ear on a cell phone. "Uh, yeah. Sure. But I don't have a pen. Can't you look it up on your superduper cop computer or something? I thought you guys could get anybody's number."

"Yeah, we can. I just wanted to know if you wanted me to have it. And now I know."

"Then, uh, call me." What in holy hell had gotten into her, Ruth wondered. Were the hooker clothes making her bold? Or was it because, Nick, the sex god, was only six inches away? Looking her up and down . . . from her tousled hair to her red velvet shoes.

She liked the way his look made her feel. Warm all over. *Hot* all over. Um, she needed to think about that. Ruth reached out to unlatch her door and swing it open. She slid halfway out of the seat, holding Tuff, who suddenly wanted to get down in a big way because he saw another mutt in front of De Lillo's.

The dog's front paws scrabbled at the air and his back paws caught in her micromini, hiking it up so high her black panties showed. Brand new—a present from Sofia that she'd added to this ridiculous outfit. Teeny-tiny. Sheer front and back. Decorated with a crystal drop that hung from a thin, black satin ribbon to right about where she was desperately pressing her thighs together.

She could drop her dog or yank down her skirt, but not both. Tuff was going nuts barking, trying to escape, so that answered that. Ruth got a better grip on him and felt her face slowly turn beet red.

Nicky looked. And looked. "Nice panties, Ruth," he said at last.

"Thanks," she gasped out.

"I like the little thing on a ribbon. What is that?"

"Ah, a decoration. A crystal."

Kept in place by the pantyhose, it did catch the eye. Then Tuff launched himself out of her arms, and she grabbed the hem of her skirt, yanking it down. Okay. She was halfway decent. Good enough. At least no one at De Lillo's had seen. "Bye-Nickyseeyathanksfortheride," she said all in one breath and went after her dog.

She bent over to grab Tuff, missed and grabbed him again. She stepped back, stumbling in the high heels and her butt slammed into a man's crotch. *Ohmigod, is he hung, whoever he is*, she thought, and turned a beetier red as she whirled around to face . . . Nick.

"Sorry. Just thought I'd help you." His low, amused voice sent a scorching heat through her. And there was a sexy edge to it that was probably making the tiny crystal decoration on her panties chime in cosmic harmony. "Tell you what. Put the pooch in the car and I'll buy you a cannoli."

A few hours later, they had eaten an entire dinner but backwards: two cannolis and three espressos at De Lillo's, followed by two bowls of the famous puttanesca at Dominick's, salad, chewy bread, and most of a bottle of good wine. By the time the check came, Nick was sitting close enough to touch her thigh. And he did, sliding a hand up her pantyhosed flesh. Ruth was on fire with lust.

"Want to come over to my place?" he asked at last, not innocently.

"Yes," replied a person that Ruth had a feeling was her.

Nick called Sofia on his cell phone, holding it far away from his ear when she shrieked at the sound of his name, then demanded to speak to Ruth, getting the explanation out of her in record time and squealing with glee.

"Ruthie, all I wanted to do was get you out of your stinkin' apartment! And you manage to run into Nicky Del Bianco? Do you know how lucky you are? I mean, he is a womanizer, but who cares, right?" Five more minutes of yapping and Sofia agreed to babysit Tuff for the night. Bambino would just have to tuck his little blue head into his speckled breast and chill until Ruth got back.

They dropped the dog off. Sofia, who'd hurriedly changed into something low-cut and tight, cooed over Tuff and cuddled him in her arms like she'd never said the dog was ugly, all for Nick's benefit. But Ruth didn't mind. She could hear Joe snoring in the den from where they stood. Sofia was too nice to invite them in, casting an appreciative glance at the arm Nick draped over Ruth's shoulders. "Have fun, you two," was all she said as she closed the door.

It was getting late and it was suddenly a lot colder. Ruth shivered as they walked back to his car. Nick let go of her, clicked open the locks with his key, and reached into the back seat to hand her his leather jacket. An old, beat-up one that he'd probably had forever—she put it around her shoulders like it was the nicest thing she'd ever worn.

Nick drove through the quiet streets of the neighborhood, not saying much, while Ruth digested . . . everything. Was he a womanizer? Well, she wanted to be womanized. Every part of her wanted to be, especially the lonesome flesh now moistening up a storm in her sheer black panties. How long had it been? She hated to think. And who had it been with? She didn't want to remember.

Nick's big hand, resting idly on the gearshift knob as he drove, would soon be sliding between her legs. He turned to smile at her. Those sensual lips would soon be kissing hers. Ruth closed her eyes and trembled. Being on fire with lust was totally fucking scary—and a lot of fun.

He turned into a driveway and parked in the garage of a new condo building. "Here we are. Ready?"

"S-sure," she said.

Next thing she knew, she was in his living room, drinking something sweet and boozy and straddling his lap. With the exception of his jacket and hers, which he'd hung up, she was fully clothed. Him too.

Nick took her glass and nuzzled her neck. "So what's your fantasy?" he whispered.

"You," she whispered back.

He stroked her back and her ass, and kissed her luxuriously. Ruth got her fingers into his dark golden hair and kissed him back, pressing herself down on his hard-on. The tight miniskirt got in the way, and she grabbed it by the hem, rolling it up so she could spread her thighs.

"Oh, man. Make yourself comfortable," he murmured. "What a body. How come I never saw you around the neighborhood after you graduated high school?"

"Because I went to NYU and lived in a dorm in downtown Manhattan."

"Why'd you come back to the Bronx?"

"Long story. Anyway, maybe you did see me around. I don't usually dress like this."

He ran his hands over her pantyhose-clad ass and thighs. "Mmm. I love it all. The skirt. The tight top and all those tiny buttons, which I'm going to undo, one by fucking one. The red velvet high heels. When I get your clothes off, those shoes are going to stay on."

"Oh, these clothes"—she tried to sound blasé—"they're not me."

He nibbled her ear. "Who cares? Pretend you're working undercover."

"Okay," she laughed. "Ruth Pirelli, undercover poet. I like the sound of that."

Nick slapped her on the butt in a friendly way. "The NYPD is looking for a few good poets."

"Oh, yeah? Sign me up."

He pulled her close into his chest and hugged her. "I was kidding. Undercover work is dangerous. And I don't want to talk shop. We were talking about . . . what were we talking about?"

"My fantasy," she said softly.

"Does it involve cops? Jesus, I hope so."

She sat up a little and began to unbutton his shirt, stroking his nipples under the fine ribbed cotton of the tank-style undershirt he wore. They were nice and dark and tight. Nick smiled sensually.

"Yeah. One cop. Who's been watching me."

He arched a brow and gave her a lazy but intrigued look. "You like to be watched, huh?" He began to undo her buttons and caressed her breasts inside the bra. "Is that a nipple ring I feel?"

"Yeah."

He groaned with pleasure. "You're full of surprises. Shy women are the wildest. So why is this cop watching you? What'd you do?"

"I didn't do anything. He lives in the building across from mine."

Nick's eyes narrowed. "For real? I'll have to kill him."

"No-oo. I'm making this up."

He pulled both breasts gently out of her bra, propping them on the soft edge of the cups and playing with her nipples. "Mm. That ring is unbelievably sexy. Any other identifying marks? Tattoos?"

"I thought you didn't want to talk shop."

"Sorry. Get back to your fantasy. I'll play with your tits and you talk."

Ruth rubbed her overflowing breasts against his face. Nick latched onto the one with the delicate nipple ring first, putting the tip of his tongue through it and tugging gently, then licking the hard tip.

"So I just got home from a club. You know, I went dancing with a few guys but no one I wanted to go home with, so I called it a night—"

"A few guys? I'll have to kill them too." He cupped both of her breasts in his big, warm hands and looked up at her blissfully.

"Nice to know I can turn you into a homicidal lunatic."

"I'm a man," Nick said. "I guard what's mine."

Make that a red-blooded Italian-American man, Ruth thought, looking down at him with admiration she couldn't hide. A native son of the beautiful Bronx and from around, just like her.

Knowing where he came from made her a whole hell of a lot more confident than usual. She pushed the other nipple into his mouth. "Shut up. So I'm feeling restless. Then I peek out the window and whaddya know—my cop is watching. I can't see him clearly but I saw the curtain at his window move a little and I get a glimpse of the outline of his body."

"Mmf." Nick got busy with her tits again.

"I want to masturbate while he watches."

He leaned his head back and tried to sit up straighter. "This could be good."

Ruth raised herself up off his lap and kneeled on the sofa

next to him, resting her arms on the back and her head on her arms. He turned to his side, taking in the new view.

She peeked at him, almost not believing that she could be so wanton. But it wasn't like she didn't know him. She had, for almost all her life, and that made all the difference.

And she wasn't lying about her fantasy. She wanted Nick to watch what she was about to do, wanted to see how hot she could get him before he begged to penetrate her. He got up with alacrity, ripping off his shirt and tossing it aside.

"Keep your pants on. This is about watching."

"Right." He kneeled in back of her.

She hooked her thumbs in the elastic waistband of her pantyhose and pulled them down about halfway down her thighs, leaving her sheer underwear where they were, still cupping her soft, round ass cheeks.

Ruth set her knees wide apart so the pantyhose were stretched tight. Nick caressed the sides of her hips, pausing to press kisses on the black chiffon of her panties, licking right through the sheer material to her swollen cunt, tasting her briefly and then going back to ass worship.

He stopped only when she reached behind with both hands and began to pull her panties down about halfway, pausing to let him fondle and stroke her ass and take a few gentle nips. Then she pulled her panties down more, really slowly, until her behind was completely bare. She could feel his breath on her naked flesh, knew he was waiting for what she would do next.

"My panties are so wet," she said softly, bringing her hands back in front of her and touching the soaked black chiffon from inside. She cupped her pussy with the same hand, then stimulated her labia with eager fingers, thrusting one in to get her juices flowing.

Nick sure as hell wasn't shy. She felt him bury his face between her thighs, thrusting his tongue in where her fingers were, working on her sensitive flesh at just her rhythm and speed.

His hands were around her ankles, and he stroked her red velvet shoes, toying with the straps like they were bondage gear, obviously enjoying giving oral pleasure to a woman who was still almost completely clothed.

Ruth knew what she looked like. She'd used mirrors to masturbate this way, looking into a little one that reflected a tall mirror in back of her, aroused by the sight of herself with a skirt pulled up, her panties stretched tautly between her thighs and her bare ass in full view, plump pussy in between. It was like watching another woman and being that woman at the same time.

Nick was licking her harder now, spreading her cheeks with strong hands. She pulled her fingers out of her pussy and stretched it open, very wide, so he could see the glistening pink.

He took his cue and shoved his tongue in deep, using it like a cock until Ruth began to moan with pleasure. He thrust his tongue again and again, giving her the hot loving she craved there, eager to be of service to her. And he stayed away from her throbbing clit, knowing instinctively that she wanted the experience to last.

After a very thorough tongue-fucking that a dyke would have been proud of—Ruth was almost in tears from the intensely pleasurable sensation of not being able to come—he pulled away, wiping his wet mouth on her warm, bare ass.

Nick got to his feet, standing over her to reach underneath and feel her breasts, overflowing the bra cups. He tugged on her nipples, handling the ringed one with particular gentleness; then kneeled on the sofa with his long, jeans-clad legs on either side of her half-bared thighs. She could feel his erect cock straining against his taut fly, pressing against the lowest part of her spine, almost between her ass cheeks, as he caressed her tits.

He reached around her waist and flipped her over like she weighed nothing, settling her on her back and grabbing her by the straps of the red velvet shoes. He lifted her legs and pulled her pantyhose and the black chiffon panties to her ankles, bunching them up so the little crystal on the ribbon was folded inside.

"I should make you stand up now," he said, his voice raw. "The way you walk in those high heels just looks so sweet—like you don't know what you're doing. Not sophisticated at all, but so sexy."

"Then let me strip. And I'll walk for you. Naked. Nothing on but the shoes," she whispered. Nick's green eyes shone with deep desire and his cock looked ready to rip through his jeans. Ruth thought with pleasure that he still hadn't been teased and pleased enough. As much as he'd seen, her peekaboo session wasn't over.

She folded her legs, knees by her shoulders, so she could unbutton the shoe straps and treat him to a good look at the juicy, bare pussy squeezed between her thighs at the same time. He toyed with the delicate curls that rimmed her inner flesh, watching her take off the shoes. He bent to lick her there with passionate tenderness, as Ruth slowly rolled the pantyhose off her feet, then the black panties, wiggling her toes.

Nick came up for air, wiping his mouth and grabbed her ankles again. He rubbed her toes sensually, easing the slight cramp from their confinement with firm pressure that shot straight to her pussy and made her writhe.

"Hold still, Ruthie." He put one of her legs over his shoulder, then bent the other one a little, licking and sucking her toes. He rested that foot on his thigh when he was done, and repeated his oral attentions on the other foot. Ruth wriggled with pleasure. Then he set that foot down too so that her thighs were widely spread and she was completely open to him. He stroked the sensitive, silky flesh on the inside of her thighs for a minute before he spoke again.

"Go ahead and masturbate," Nick said. "I want to watch. I want to learn exactly what you like." He gazed dreamily into her eyes until Ruth slid her hands down her body, undoing the last of the tiny buttons on her top and pulling it open but keeping it on. Her skirt was rucked up around her waist—below it, everything was bared to him.

She took her clit between her middle finger and her thumb, pulling it up from the slick flesh that enfolded it.

"Want me to suck that?"

"No," she whispered. "I don't want to come yet." But she did want to turn him on even more. She rolled it, even pinched it, and heard him draw in a ragged breath. He was staring hard at her pussy. He watched her masturbate for a little while longer, then took her hand and sucked her hot juice off her fingers.

"Get up," he said hoarsely. He picked up the red velvet shoes from the floor. "And put these back on and do that strip you promised me."

"Mmm," was all she said. Ruth sat up, feeling deliciously woozy, and bent over to strap on the shoes, standing with unsteady grace. He grabbed her skirt and pulled it down, flopping back into the sofa cushions.

"Oh, yeah. I can see your pussy from here. Go, girl."

Her long, dark hair was mussed and half-hiding her face as she reached around behind and unzipped the skirt. With a seductiveness that amazed her, Ruth slid the micromini down over her hips and stepped out of it. Then she slipped her unbuttoned top down around the tops of her arms, using it to squeeze her breasts higher out of her bra.

She turned around, letting him look at her ass. Nick didn't grab, just reached for it. His hands were big enough to clasp each cheek. He spread them while she stood there. She knew he was looking at that tight little hole in between. Ruth let the top slide off her arms to the floor and arched backward, letting him support her with his hands on her spread cheeks, and unhooking her bra.

Naked, feeling sexed up, she just stood there, teetering on

those red velvet platforms. Then she twisted her hips and tried to turn around, but he wouldn't let her.

Okay, she thought. Have it your way. Ruth bent over at the waist, sliding her fingers into her dripping wet pussy again, knowing he could see exactly what she was doing.

"Get back on the sofa and do that," Nick moaned. "Face to the wall, ass to me." She obeyed, amused by how fast he moved to get behind her again.

She got comfortable on her knees, working her fingers into her pussy again, making him crazy with watching. Then she reached completely around and inserted one slick finger into her asshole. Just the tip. Working nice and slow, penetrating the tight ring of puckered flesh.

He gasped. "Oh, no. I'm about to come in my pants." She heard him unzip but she didn't turn around, just pulled her finger out of her ass with a soft pop. He shucked his jeans and everything else.

Nick rested his hands on her bare ass, placing his legs to either side of hers the way he'd done before. "Reach back, Ruthie. Touch my cock. I'm too big to go in your ass. But thanks for the show."

She did. The shaft that bobbed between her legs was long and heavy, and smooth as silk. She curled over a little to give him long strokes from base to the head, catching the first hot drop of cum by accident in her palm.

Rocked by lust, he grabbed her ass for support. "Condom," he muttered. "Scuse me." He let go, looking somewhere for the necessary article while she waited, being wickedly patient and swaying her bare ass, aware that she had excited him to the max.

Ruth wanted to shove that huge cock inside her, and get her pussy pounded by an Italian stallion in the worst way. She rested her face on her crossed arms, listening the foil packet being ripped open, and the quick, soft sound of a stiff penis being sheathed with practiced skill.

He came back to her. Nick positioned the plum-size head right at her labia, grabbing her buttocks again, prepared to thrust.

But Ruth beat him to it. She pushed hard against the wall back at him, taking him into her so deeply the pleasure made her cry out. She banged her ass against his taut groin again and again, and it took all his strength to hang on.

And all his willpower not to come first. But when Ruth curled over and began to rub her pussy with wild abandon, he could feel her fingertips just brushing his big balls.

With each touch of her hand, his scrotum tightened. Her flesh, his flesh, hot and slick, hard and soft, moved with turbo-charged speed, until he held her hips motionless, his fingers digging into her, and cried out in a strong orgasm. And a second afterward, so did she.

2

Three weeks later...

Nicky ushered her into the Palm Hall at the Auguste Hotel, his hand gently resting between her shoulder blades. The sensation of his touch went right to . . . the tiny crystal decoration on her panties. Ruth considered them lucky. Sofia had had to agree.

For this date, the cousins had gone shopping and maxed out Ruth's plastic. They'd returned from Loehmann's with bags full of drop-dead outfits guaranteed to thrill Nicky Del Bianco and have him eating out of Ruth's newly manicured hand.

She gazed up at the high ceilings of the Palm Hall for a second and said a silent wow. The paneled room had tall potted palms that offered strategic hiding places for men in expensive suits and their generally younger dates with uniformly blond highlights. Every single one of the women eyed Nicky, and then shot Ruth a jealous look.

She looked back, cool and calm. *He's mine.* She stood a little straighter and Nicky's hand stayed right where it was. On the back of the cream-colored bolero jacket that covered her black velvet afternoon cocktail dress. With long black velvet gloves to match. *Hoo-hah*, Sofia had said when she found them on a sale table. *The perfect touch.*

Ruth had added a pair of elegant black patent leather stilettos, suitable for kicking off and playing footsie under a damask tablecloth or in a deluxe hotel bed.

"Can you afford this place on a detective's salary?" she whispered to him.

"For you, yeah." He brushed a kiss over her cheekbone and the other women's eyes flashed Godzilla sparks. Yeah. Pure envy. Ruth was sure of it. She parted her red, red lips in a smile as she turned toward the approaching maitre d'.

The men shook hands and Nicky slapped him on the shoulder, light and friendly. "Hey, Henry. Two for lunch." Obviously they knew each other. Nicky had said that he knew the assistant manager too, Eduardo Fernandez, a Dominican he called Mr. Teeth.

Who was also coming over, unless she missed her guess. Mr. Teeth was an older guy, tall, with silver hair and bronzed skin. She spotted the discreet badge on his dark suit before he got to them. He shook Nick's hand next and bowed just a little to her. Aww. Ruth was a sucker for Latin charm. So long as she didn't have to get her hand kissed.

"Henry, Eduardo—this is Ruth Pirelli."

"So. This why you been missing our poker games. Now I understand," Eduardo said, favoring her with a devastatingly sexy smile. She understood the nickname.

"Hi, guys," she said shyly.

The maitre d' exchanged a few murmured words with Nick, then led the way to a table for two, away from the others. "Okay with you?" Nick said.

"Yeah, sure," she answered nervously. The maitre d' pulled out her chair. Oh, hell. How did this work again? With her luck, she'd end up on her butt. She took a deep breath and went for it, sliding into the chair as Henry pushed it forward. Perfect. She hadn't flubbed it. Maybe she even looked like she belonged here.

Ruth put her handbag on the white damask tablecloth and took off her gloves, wiggling her fingertips to cool them off. The gloves were very *Breakfast at Tiffany's* but this was lunch at the Auguste, which seemed to be a pretty sedate place.

She inspected her flashy fingernails, feeling a little self-conscious. Maybe they were too flashy, she thought nervously. Sofia had talked her into the French tips. She quickly hid her hands in her lap. Nicky sat down across from her and looked into her eyes.

"You're gorgeous, you know that? You make every other woman in this room look like nothing."

She blushed and picked up her napkin, spreading it across her lap. Prim and proper. His open admiration turned her on. He made no secret of wanting her, but since their first date and what happened after he hadn't put the pressure on so much that she was nervous.

What he had done was come around. Lots of times. He always called first and he called often. Sofia was right: when a guy was interested, he put you on his speed dial. And it gave her a chance to get out of her sweats and sneaks and into something nice, so he could fuck her silly in it.

Nick liked to stay in touch through the day, not to keep tabs on her but to make her laugh and blow off steam himself, telling her about the crazy crap that went on at the precinct, so long as it didn't involve an active investigation. The ugly side of being an NYPD detective he left out. For which she was grateful. Ruth read the *Post*; she didn't need to know. She'd seen his name printed in it once, something to do with a long-unsolved mob murder that was finally going to trial, and felt a flash of pride.

Nick unfolded his napkin too, and a waiter came by with two huge leather-bound menus ornamented with tassels, which he presented with a flourish.

"Thanks. Give us a couple of minutes, okay?"

The waiter nodded and withdrew. Ruth picked something that sounded safe and familiar, and Nicky decided on the same thing. They chatted, ate, chatted some more over coffee and dessert . . . until he reached for the cell phone vibrating in his inside jacket pocket. He looked at the number and shook his head.

"Do you have to go? I can catch the D train home—the subway stop's just a few blocks away. I can say hello to the carriage horses on Central Park South on my way there." Might as well make the best of it, she thought a little unhappily.

"Yeah, they love the crudités. Especially the carrot sticks." He didn't seem eager to leave and he was eying her in a way that made her feel hot all over. "Actually, I think I can safely ignore that call. It's Ralphie the rookie. Let someone else check his homework."

"Oh. Okay then. So what happens next?"

"I was wondering—if you wanted to spend the night here."

In the middle of taking a sip of coffee, she almost choked on it, thinking irrationally that he meant *here*. As in under the potted palms.

"I got us a suite. For tonight. Eduardo pulled a few strings. View of the park, room service, the whole nine. Up to you."

Ruth looked at him with surprise. "A suite at the Auguste costs thousands of dollars a night. You don't have the money for that."

"No, I don't," he said easily.

She thought it over for a good five seconds. No doubt there was a reasonable explanation and she was about to hear it. She would have to be crazy to say no. Ruth made a mental note to call Sofia and ask her to take Tuff for the night.

"We broke a jewel-theft ring here a few years back," he said at last. "The management of the Auguste still appreciates it. When there's an empty suite that can't be booked for the night, all Eduardo has to do is ask them and tell us. There's a few perks to this job."

"I read about that case. What was it, like ten million dollars in diamonds that went missing? I didn't know you handled that one."

He grinned. "So. Want to go up?"

Ruth put down her handbag and black velvet gloves on a foyer table and looked around. "Oh, Nicky. This is awesome. I've never been in a four-star hotel room—I mean suite." She slipped off her jacket and hung it up.

He gave her a wolfish smile. "And we didn't even have to put up with suspicious looks from the desk clerk. Eduardo took care of that."

She kicked off her stilettos. The carpet underfoot was seriously thick and soft—she padded around on it, then looked up to see him smiling at her. "Nice. Cushy. Lucky you. All these friends in a swanky hotel."

Nicky was flopped down on the sofa, legs apart but not so he looked like he was pretending to be a player or anything. Just getting comfortable. "You look fuckin' fantastic in that black dress. My undercover angel." He stretched his arms out along the back of the sofa. "You know, you really would be good at that."

"Yeah, right," she snorted. "I don't do dangerous. I walk my dog, I live my life."

"I was just saying, that's all. We had this discussion. I wouldn't put you in danger. I like you too much." He gave her a lazy, sensual look that took her in from head to toe. "But I think you could use some excitement. C'mon over here when you get done testing the carpet."

Ruth froze. His big hand rested on one sprawled thigh. She glanced at it and then at his crotch. He definitely had an erection already. A big one.

"Not interested?" He seemed amused.

"No—I mean, yeah. I am. But—"

"Intimidated by your surroundings?"

She wriggled her toes in the carpet. "A little. I'm not used to this. But I can fake it."

"You don't fake anything. But I had to find that out for myself." He gave her a look she couldn't quite read. "Did I tell you I even asked a couple of the guys what you were all about? Nice to know you didn't get with anyone from our neighborhood."

"And just how the hell do you know that?"

He laughed but in a nice way. "No info on the grapevine. And no one would confess to anything."

"Well, I never dated anyone you would know. I don't think," she added hastily.

Okay, so she hadn't done a whole hell of a lot of dating in the last five years. Sofia hadn't been too far off the mark with that you-have-a-complex remark. Dating just seemed like a waste of time, and sex—well, Ruth didn't see any reason to hop into bed with someone who wasn't interesting enough to talk to.

But Nick had changed all that. Just sitting on the sofa, he radiated an ultra-male sexuality that made her pussy throb. She knew if she took one more step in his direction she would be clinging to him like Little Miss Magnet to Mr. Fridge. She took the step.

"Keep going, beautiful. I don't bite." He beckoned her with one finger. Ruth almost tripped over her own feet and landed in his lap. He caught her and settled her bottom between his thighs.

She could feel his big cock getting instantly bigger. Wow. All right. She didn't even try to pull her rumpled-up dress down. Nick bent his head for a peek. "Oh yeah. Those panties. Unforgettable."

Ruth smiled when he brushed his lips along the side of her neck, and made one of her earrings jingle. "Want me to take them off?"

"No," he murmured. "I think women look sexier when they keep a few things on. Earrings. Panties. Shoes." His roving hand slipped up under her dress and found the elastic waist of her pantyhose. "But you could lose these for a start."

Ruth arched in his lap, helping him pull off the pantyhose. She folded her bare legs up to get them off her feet and handed them to him. He stuffed them into his pants pocket. "Taking a souvenir? I'm not walking out of this hotel looking like the big bad wolf ate my new clothes. Everyone will know what we were doing."

"I'll give them back, I promise. Just didn't want to lose them." He rummaged in his other pocket and pulled out a clean handkerchief. "Here. Get the lipstick off. I don't want to look like a clown after I kiss you."

She rubbed it off with swift strokes and put the handkerchief on a side table. He slid his hand into the lightly boned bodice of her dress, fondling her breasts. Ruth let him capture her soft moan of pleasure with his mouth, on hers again, kissing her for all he was worth.

His tongue was sweet and soft, tasting faintly of chocolate cake and coffee. The man was better than dessert, better than anything. He stroked her hair, pushing it away from her face so he could hold her chin and make the kiss more intense.

She opened to his exploring tongue, let him nip her wet lower lip, and kissed him back. Her hand moved from his shoulder, caressing his bicep, and then over to his chest. She flicked open the buttons of his shirt with her long fingernails. One by one.

"Oo. Hello, pecs." She stroked the golden skin of his bare chest, playing with the dark, springy hair between his tight nipples, tracing a French-tipped fingernail over one.

"I like those nails," he said softly. "Sexy. When you were holding that menu I was thinking about you touching yourself with those beautiful hands." He patted the front of her panties. "Right here. Under that little thing." He took the crystal decoration between finger and thumb, tugging gently on the thin ribbon until he pulled her panties down a little in front. "Do it. I want to watch."

Ruth hesitated for a fraction of a second . . . then slid her fingers into the springy curls. She heard him draw in a ragged breath. "Oh, yeah." She wriggled in his lap and spread her legs wider, leaning back into the strong arm that curved around her. He pulled her panties down a little bit more.

She stroked between her labia, surprised by how wet she was already. God, who wouldn't be in Nicky Del Bianco's arms, about to get naked and thoroughly fucked? His green gaze was fixed on her crotch, watching her finger slide in and out. In and out. Her clit was throbbing and she touched it gently.

"Afternoon delight. Here we go," Nick said softly. He shifted so he could see everything she was doing, easing her back onto the pillows that lay against the sofa arm. She reached out to touch his cock, still trapped in his pants, but he captured her hand and put it back on her pussy.

"No . . . not yet. Just keep touching yourself . . ." He didn't finish the sentence as he yanked her panties farther down, bringing her knees together. Her hand was caught between her legs by the sudden motion. "Yeah. Leave it there."

Nick scrambled out from underneath and stood up, breathing heavily. He pulled out her pantyhose from his pocket and grabbed her ankles, tying them together as she fell back into the soft seat cushions of the sofa. He kneeled next to her, gently folding her legs so her knees were up by her shoulders. Her pussy was fully exposed to him, swollen and squeezed by the position she was in. Nick stroked her hand, then licked the fingers that were on her pussy and clit.

She rocked on her back, extremely aroused by the suddenness of his taking charge and instinctively aware of how excited he was.

Ruth loved this game: being caught in the act of masturbating by a dominant lover who wanted to watch. With her dress up and panties pulled down to her knees. Ankles tied and bottom up. And her hand held tightly between her clasped thighs, stroking her slick folds and her tense clit.

She could feel his tongue licking over her fingers and in between, inside her pussy. He thrust it in, over and over. Ruth tipped her head to one side, totally into what he was doing but wanting to admire the powerful body kneeling beside her, loving the strength of the man who was giving her so much pleasure.

Nick lifted his head and just about ripped off his unbuttoned shirt. Her free hand reached out to caress his bare chest and he didn't push it away until he stood up to shuck his pants and briefs at the same time, stepping out of them and standing proudly naked.

She reached out to touch his tight balls and stroke as much of his huge cock as she could reach. He let her, looking down, looking like he enjoyed the pretty hand that encircled his cock and teased his balls. Ruth ran a hand over the sensitive flesh on the insides of his thighs and up to his groin. Nick trembled and his cock bobbed like he was going to shoot his load. He grabbed it hard and groaned. "Not yet . . . not yet."

But his grip squeezed out a few drops of cum. She opened her mouth and licked her lips, looking straight at him. "Give me a taste, Nicky," she whispered.

"You're not shy at all, are you?" he said. "Not when you get down and dirty." He bent his big body over her and put the head of his cock to her waiting lips. Ruth darted out her tongue and cleaned the tender hole for him, licking up the clear, hot cum as he gasped.

"No," she said softly. "Not any more. You taste so good, Nicky."

He let go of his cock and straightened up, undoing the panty-hose knotted around her ankles and pulling her panties off the rest of the way. That left her dress. No bra, not with a boned bodice. She struggled with the zipper and slid part way out of the dress lying down, then stretched up her arms to let him pull off. He did the honors, not very carefully. "Easy, big guy."

He wasn't listening. He cupped her bare breasts in his hands and dropped to his knees on the thick carpet, sucking one and fondling the other. Ruth stroked his messed-up hair, letting him press his face into her flesh and satisfy his hunger. Her breasts weren't all that big but her nipples were long, and the foreplay made them even longer. Nicky moved quickly from one to the other, pulling each nipple into his mouth, circling his eager tongue around the sensitive tip.

He straightened up, still on his knees, and pushed her back so she was lying flat. Her thighs fell open and he twisted his torso sideways to give her head, plunging his tongue into her pussy until she clutched the sofa arm behind her head, writhing.

Nick buried his face between her legs, worshipping her female flesh with his mouth, not holding back. Then he pulled back and squatted on his haunches. She wished she could see his balls hanging down under his huge cock, but her imagination was almost as good. She might just have to make him masturbate too and let her watch while he lubed himself and stroked his cock fast and hard, cupping his own balls as his cum pulsed out in hot, strong spurts. The thought almost made her lose her mind, and it was a minute before she realized he was talking to her.

"Touch yourself again. Pull on that clit with those long fingernails. Pinch it. Like you were disciplining another woman. Leading her around by her clit because she wanted you to."

"And you were watching," she whispered, understanding the fantasy.

She spread her labia completely apart, watching his eyes widen at the sight. Then she held her clitoris with the edge of her long nails, enjoying the delicately sharp sensation that she could control. The little ridge of sensitive flesh was slippery but her nails held it.

"Now you're showing it to me. And telling me to lick it."

"Lick it. Just the tip."

He brought his head down at an angle and stuck out his tongue, flicking it over her clit tip very rapidly and lightly.

Ruth dug her nails in and cried out. Focused on that one tiny point of extreme pleasure, she came hard. He pulled her hand away and put his soft mouth over her throbbing flesh, heightening the incredible sensation with tender skill. She heard herself cry out again, as if from a long way off, and opened her eyes when he got up. He was rolling on a condom that he must have had at the ready. Thank you, she thought, drunk with lust. She hadn't even thought about it. Nicky was the best, that was all there was to it. Then suddenly he was above her on all fours, throwing the extra cushions to the floor.

"Put your legs up. I gotta get deep."

"I want you to," she almost sobbed. She lifted her legs and pushed her dripping, totally satisfied pussy against the head of his cock. With a half-strangled shout, he plunged in, ramming up to the hilt inside her. She was so aroused, it didn't matter how hard he fucked her, huge as he was.

Nick's big shoulders kept her legs pressed up. He didn't put his full weight on her, though, holding himself up with his muscular arms as he banged her. His balls bumped her tender pussy right under his thrusting shaft and she rocked with each thrust, consumed again by fierce desire. He moaned, shuddering and sweating, as he thrust faster. His groin tightened and he came down hard one last time, ejaculating so strongly that she felt it. He gasped, his eyes closed, in a sexual trance as he finished. She looked up in wonder. Nick Del Bianco was a big, hot, healthy animal.

And he's mine, she thought again. *All mine*. They collapsed . . . and slept.

Ruth woke in the middle of the night, not knowing where she was and feeling a flash of panic. She sat bolt upright in the huge hotel bed and peered around the shadowy room and into the adjoining space beyond. A flash of movement caught her eye and all of a sudden Nicky filled the doorway, silhouetted in warm light, wearing a thick white bathrobe that was open at the front, the sash ends hanging down to his knees.

Then she remembered. Everything. "Hey, Nicky," she said shyly.

"Hey back, beautiful. Sorry I woke you."

"It's all right. What time is it?"

He looked at the nightstand clock before she did. "About two. You've been asleep for hours."

"Guess I needed it," she said lightly. "Whatcha doing?"

"Looking at Central Park. Come and see." He stretched out a hand. "The carriage horses all went home and the streets are empty. Couple of cops, yawning their heads off in front of the Plaza. That's about it for excitement."

"That's okay," she said, getting up. "All the excitement wore me out. Poor you. I hope there was something good on TV."

He enfolded her in a huge terrycloth hug that felt fabulous. Ruth buried her nose in his bathrobe and then moved to his chest, nuzzling him.

"You showered. You smell good."

He nodded. "And I shaved. You should see the toiletries kit

they provide in these suites. It has everything, not just soap and shampoo. Massage oil. Pedicure kit. Condoms."

She kissed the spot over his heart. "I was wondering where you got that."

Nick laughed. "You know, I keep one in my wallet but it's been there a while. Did I ever tell you I named it after an old girlfriend?"

Ruth couldn't help but pout a little. "Do I wanna know?"

"Her name was Hope." He tweaked her nose. "Don't sulk. I'm teasing you, dopey."

She slid her arm around his waist and got as much of herself as she could inside the open front of his bathrobe. He pulled the lapels together and walked her backwards to the window, stepping carefully between her much smaller feet with his big ones, and keeping her pretty much covered, except for her ass, which stuck out.

Nicky patted it. "Hiya, sweet cheeks. How nice to see you." He stopped and picked up a cashmere throw that had been draped artistically over the back of an armchair. "Here. You can use this for a sarong."

Ruth slipped out from his robe, shivering a little even though the suite was warm. She tied the throw over her chest, enjoying the grin he gave her and the extra pats he bestowed on her cashmere-draped boobs. "Mmm. Nice and soft. Looks good too. You really have style, you know that?"

She shook her head. "Huh-uh. Sofia does. She's teaching me, though."

"Then you learn fast. C'mon, let's enjoy the view." He walked ahead and stood in front of a floor-to-ceiling window, looking out at Central Park by night. Here on the southeast corner of Fifth Ave and 60th Street, there was always some traffic, even in the wee hours of the morning. A lone taxi shot down the middle lane, marked with diamonds for fire trucks and ambulances.

It was rare not to hear a siren somewhere in the night in New York. But there wasn't one. Ruth looked down. The meandering paths of Central Park were lit at night with old-fashioned streetlamps. At this season, they were partially hidden by tall, leafy trees that cast deep black shadows. From this height, the lamps looked like floating, glowing dots of bluish white.

"Pretty, huh? Good thing neither of us has to go to work tomorrow."

"Yeah." She turned around and noticed the room-service trolley she'd missed seeing when he'd had her wrapped up in his bathrobe. "Where'd that come from?"

"I figured you'd be hungry. Eduardo left word with the night shift manager to send some stuff up. Shrimp cocktail. Lobster salad. Cold cuts." He lifted a flaccid slice of pinkish baloney with a fork and looked at it with disgust. "Is this what you get at a four-star hotel? Forget the cold cuts. But the rest looks good. And there's green salad and fresh fruit. And more chocolate cake to help grow big hips twelve ways."

She pressed her lips together, then opened them to speak. "I don't want big hips."

"Hey, I'm Italian. I happen to *like* big hips. Have some goddamn cake if you want cake." He poured himself a glass of wine and stuck a shrimp in his mouth, wiggling the tail at her.

"You're not eating it," Ruth pointed out, laughing at how silly he looked.

"Protein first. Then salad. That way I can fill up on good stuff before I devour too much cake."

"Sounds like a good plan."

He ate the shrimp and put the tail into an ashtray. "I learned it the hard way. My mother loves to cook. Every Sunday she makes fresh pasta and shovels it into everybody who shows up. When everybody passes out in a carbo coma, she's happy. Italian women are like that."

"I'm not. I don't cook."

He shrugged and took another shrimp, waving it to make his next point. "That's okay. My mother would say you couldn't, whether you did or didn't. You'll see. I was thinking of bringing you to meet her. You up for that?"

Ruth steeled herself. "Meet the mama? That's a big step."

"Well, we don't have to think about it now. C'mon, eat something. Then I'll give you a bath and a massage. Or a massage, then a bath. You pick."

"Twist my arm, Nicky Del Bianco." She walked over to the trolley and filled up a small plate, trying a forkful of lobster salad first.

"Tasty, huh? Chow down. I wanna get you into a bubble bath, get you out, and start all over again."

She slipped the fork out of her mouth nice and slow, and licked the tines for good measure. "When I'm ready. I wake up slow."

Nicky finally got around to the chocolate cake, and cut a piece, taking it over to the sofa and turning on the TV, flicking through the channels with the remote. "Okay, okay. I can take a hint. Wanna watch the news?"

"No." She finished the lobster salad.

"How about that women's channel where someone's always having a baby?"

"Hell, no." She gobbled the greens.

"Korean soap opera?"

Ruth started in on the fruit salad. "Don't think so." The melon balls and strawberry halves disappeared in a few bites.

"The sex fiend show?" He turned to see her showing him the empty plate.

"I'm done eating. Let's make our own. Starring you and me." She headed for the bathroom, untying the cashmere sarong and draping it over the armchair again. He caught up with her just in time to grab her ass but she smacked his hands away.

"Holy cow. I've never seen a bathroom this big. It even has a chaise."

He picked up the information placard on it and read aloud. "Enjoy our deluxe bath chaise and its exclusive vibrating option. Experience the ultimate in comfort and personal pleasure. Hey, I have an idea—"

"I want that bath you promised first."

Nicky tossed the placard aside. "Then get in the tub."

Ruth stepped in, pulling her long hair up and tying it in a sloppy knot.

"You can tie your hair in a knot? Cool," he said admiringly. "I didn't know you could do that."

"I'm a woman of many talents. Okay, it won't stay up for long. Let's do this fast."

Nick turned on the taps and adjusted the faucet gizmo. Jets of pulsing water shot out of a hanging, steel-tubed shower nozzle, which twisted and writhed, spraying every which way. It was nice and warm, but Ruth squealed anyway.

"Spread 'em," he said, laughing. He pulsed the spray between her legs, grabbing a bar of soap with his other hand and soaping up her crotch. Then he let the water rinse it all away. It was deliciously soothing. Ruth turned around, bending over wantonly and letting him spray her buttocks and in between.

"You're getting me hard," he said.

She gave him a flirty glance over her shoulder. "Are you complaining?"

"Not about the way you look, pretty girl, with your hair up like that and your face all pink, getting your bottom squeaky clean."

She wiggled it at him. "Look your fill."

He gave her a slap. "Done."

Ruth turned around. "Now do my tits."

"You're insatiable."

She took the shower nozzle from him and let it pulse hard onto her nipples. "That's how I like it. Intense. Up close."

His green eyes got a dreamy look as he watched her stimulate herself again. She took the soap and lathered up luxuriously, sluicing the warm water over her breasts, rinsing between her legs again when the foam caught in her tangled pubic curls, and then did each leg, posing like a pin-up.

His huge cock jutted out from the open front of his bathrobe. "I could watch you do that all night," he said. His voice was low and a little rough.

Ruth shivered. "Uh-uh. I'm cold. Throw me a towel."

"Here ya go."

She caught it and rubbed herself dry and warm again, then tossed it on the tiled floor and stepped out. "What were you saying about a massage?"

"Coming up. Lie down on that thing. Face down." He waved expansively at the chaise. "I think we need to explore that exclusive vibrating option."

Refreshed and rested, she felt ready for pretty much anything. "God, I love hotels. Not that I've ever been in one like this."

"Stick with me, babe." He fluffed out a folded towel over the chaise for her to lie down on, sat down on the raised end, and patted the longer, flat part.

Ruth looked at him, then at the chaise. She put one leg all the way over to the floor on the other side, then pivoted and lay down, straddling the chaise, her feet on the floor and her ass spread open. She looked over her shoulder at Nicky, who was eying everything on display with undisguised lust. "Go ahead and look. Gets you hot, doesn't it?"

"Yeah," he growled.

"Then get the lotion."

He rose and grabbed the bottle, shaking a big dollop of it into his palm.

"Let it warm up first," she instructed.

Nicky sighed but he waited at least a minute, then rubbed the lotion over her back in long, smooth strokes. "How's that for the royal treatment?"

"Mmmm," she sighed with contentment.

He kept on rubbing, getting into it, doing her neck between finger and thumb, making sensual circles down her spine and up again, releasing the muscular tension of falling asleep in a strange bed. Her skin was soft and smooth by the time he was finished rubbing her back, and not oily at all.

Her eyes were closed but not her senses. Ruth felt him add two more dollops of lotion, one on each side of her ass, and rub them in slowly. Very slowly. Squeezing and parting her cheeks with loving care.

"Love that little hole. Looks tempting. And tight."

"Mmm."

"That's not a yes and not a no. But I'm not going to try. I'm too big for you there."

"Just keep rubbing." He did. She began to undulate, pressing her pussy into the thick towel underneath.

"Ruth, please. I'm only human. You're driving me crazy here."

"That's why I'm making you look. I want to know if I can trust you."

He groaned and growled, but he did her bidding. When he rested his hands on her ass cheeks for a moment, she didn't say anything, just enjoyed the warmth of them, and the strength that flowed from his flesh to hers. Very quickly, she lifted up and arched her back, looking over her shoulder at him. His expression was different, not mellow at all. More like he was fighting for self-control.

"Go ahead then," she said softly. "Touch me there. But don't go in. All you get to do is think about it."

Nick let out his breath and took his hands off her bare ass.

She settled down and relaxed, watching him dip a finger into the lotion. He cupped one cheek again, spreading her slightly with it, and treated her to an anal massage, obeying her wish to not penetrate her there. She hid her face in her folded arms, knowing that not giving him everything he wanted was making him superhot. And probably superstiff.

"Mm-hm. That's enough," she said, her voice muffled.

He stopped and pulled a tissue from the box with a whisking sound, getting the lotion off his finger. "Look, but don't touch. Touch, but don't penetrate. Tell me where you get your ideas. That might have been the hottest five minutes of my life."

Ruth sat up, still straddling the chaise, and stretched. "I enjoyed it," she said nonchalantly. "Quite a treat." She stood up, her ass in his face, and stepped over the chaise again, turning to face him. His erection was straining up against his belly button, she noticed with pleasure.

"How about a treat for me?"

"What would that be?"

He looked back into the suite and pointed to her stiletto heels, lying where she'd left them. "Those. Put them on. Fucking a woman in high heels and nothing else is great. From behind."

"Can I trust you?" She smiled.

"Yeah." He ran his hands over her bare legs and planted a kiss on her springy, clean pubic curls. "You know you can. I was a good boy, wasn't I?

She sashayed back into the suite and bent over to pick up the shoes she'd taken off several hours ago. And her black velvet dress. If she went home with wrinkled clothes to pick up her dog, Sofia would never shut up. And Ruth wasn't going to share one word of her awesome night of lust with her inquisitive cousin.

With the shoes in her hand, she managed to hang up the dress in the hall closet, glancing at Nick when she shut the door. "What are you grinning at?"

"You look so domestic. Picking up your clothes, hanging them up. You'll be getting out the ironing board next."

Ruth snorted. "That'll be the day. I just don't want to go home looking like a total slut on the subway."

"Not gonna happen."

She cocked her head and put her hands on her hips, shoes and all. "What are you going to do about it? Send me home to the Bronx on a parade float?"

He got up, his erection down to a semi but still an impressive sight. "Good idea. Hadn't thought of that. Ten tons of crepe paper ruffles and you in a giant clamshell, all pink and pearly, waving to the guidos."

She held up the stilettos. "And wearing these."

"Yeah," he said enthusiastically. "Put them on."

Ruth slid her feet into them, teetered, and then squatted down to get the thin straps over the back of her heels. Her breasts squeezed over her knees and Rick squatted down right in front of her, sucking a nipple and trying to keep her steady at the same time. They both went over, laughing. He got up first and pulled her up, yanking her to him for a long, luxurious kiss. "We never did try out the vibrating option, Ruthie. C'mon . . . be my fantasy again. I can't believe how hot you get me."

She clasped him and stroked him to full hardness, whispering against his lips, "Then let's do it." She led the way back into the bathroom, leading him by his cock just for fun. The steam had cleared out and Ruth could see her face in the mirror again. She picked up a natural bristle hairbrush, another gift from the management, and began brushing her hair.

Nicky investigated the control panel, switching on the vibration at a low setting. "All systems go. Have a seat. Ladies ride free." He spread a fresh towel for her and slipped off the bathrobe.

Ruth straddled the couch again but she sat up this time. He picked up the hairbrush she'd set down and sat behind her, running it through her hair with the same long, even strokes he'd used to rub her back. Bliss.

The very slight vibration between her spread legs was sensual but nowhere near as good as having a big, strong guy brush her hair. Nicky stopped for a minute, running his fingers through the glossy strands. "Like silk," he murmured. "And it smells so good." He buried his nose in it, then reached around to caress her breasts.

"I thought you just wanted to fuck me from behind."

She could feel him smile into her hair. "I do. But all this girl stuff—long hair and soft tits—has to be appreciated first." He scooted closer to her on the chaise, letting his erection rest in the cleft between her buttocks. "Do you like the vibration? Do you use one to get off?"

"Sometimes I used to," she admitted, bowing her head when he lifted the heavy hair off her neck and kissed her nape. He held her in a loose embrace, fondling her breasts and tugging at her long nipples, playing with the ring on one that he liked so much. Without her seeing him, the power of his very masculine body, so much larger than her own, seemed mysteriously strong. The deep voice vibrating in her ear made the vibration between her legs stronger still.

Ruth shifted, not wanting to have an almost accidental orgasm. He wanted a hot bitch in high heels, bent over and spread, begging for cock, he was going to get one.

The intensity of their desire for each other seemed almost surreal. The luxuriousness of the hotel suite, the feeling of being apart from the ordinary world, alone in the night with each other, only added to the strangely sensual feeling that enveloped her.

"I don't want to come yet," she whispered to him. "Don't think about satisfying me. You already did that. When you washed me—and massaged me—it made me want you all over again but I can wait. Now you come first."

She moved her leg over the side of the chaise and swung around to face him partway. Nicky cradled her in his arms. "I think I understand what you mean. Either way. If that's your pleasure, then it's mine." He kissed her long and deep, and Ruth felt herself go limp. Her thighs fell open and he put two thick fingers at the opening of her pussy, still holding her securely in his other arm. The clean flesh didn't have much lube and he had to push a little. He stopped about a half inch in. She braced her stiletto heels against the floor and lifted up, spreading her thighs even wider and making a submissive display of her labia.

"Good girl," Nick murmured. "Show yourself. Show me." Her sweet juice began to flow at the sound of his voice and he pushed his fingers into her all the way. "You like to be fucked, don't you?"

"Yes," she whispered. "By you. Only you." She felt the slight but constant vibration of the chaise right through his body and wondered if he'd forgotten it was on.

He nodded, bending his head to kiss the hair he had brushed so gently. "Tell me what you're thinking about. Tell me your fantasy."

"That you're spanking me," she whispered. "I need it and I want it and I asked for it."

"Okay." He kept on fingerfucking her.

"But lightly."

She felt him smile against her hair.

"Got it." He withdrew his fingers and reached for a rolled towel, which he placed by the side of the chaise. "Turn over. And kneel down. Lie over the chaise crossways. Don't touch yourself. This is going to be very gentle discipline but you have to obey."

She did, kneeling on the rolled towel and crossing her legs at the ankles.

"Good girl. Now put your head in my lap." He stretched

out his leg and guided her head down onto his thigh so all she could see was his cock and balls. "Look but don't touch. You asked for a light spanking and I want you to see just how hot it makes me to do that to you. My hand or the hairbrush?"

"Your hand," she whispered. When they were skin to skin, the feeling was awesome, like nothing she had ever experienced.

He lifted her hair off her neck and draped it over his thigh. Then he picked up the hairbrush and ran it through her hair a few more times. The contact was even more sensual than before, perhaps because she was now more open to him, choosing to play a role that let him be dominant.

He set the brush aside and stroked her buttocks softly. Ruth trembled. She had never asked a boyfriend to spank her, had never trusted anyone that much, had never wanted anyone else to do it. But she had fantasized about it.

And then along came Nick, alpha male. And she was doing it for real. Or rather, he was doing it to her. Bliss.

He stroked her back several times and then paused. She looked at his stiff cock and his balls, drawn up tight to the base of the shaft, and closed her eyes, holding that image in her mind as she pressed her face into his muscular thigh. His hand came down on her buttocks with a slap that left a refreshing, very slight sting. He did it again. And again. Ruth was in heaven. She held very still. It was everything she had read about and more. His intent focus on her. The sensation itself. Knowing that he was looking at her glowing ass cheeks and getting excited by what she'd permitted him to do, asked him to do.

"That's three," he said. "Do you want more?"

"Yes, please."

"Then get up. Straddle the chair. Back to me."

Dreamy-eyed and so stimulated the inside of her thighs were wet, she sat back on her haunches and looked at him. His jaw was set and his green eyes were on fire with hot, male lust.

"Be good. Do what I say."

He helped her get up, wobbling a little on the high heels she'd forgotten she was still wearing. The vulnerability of her stance or the shoes themselves seemed to provoke something in him, desire from a darker place.

He drew in a deep breath and controlled himself, caressing the sides of her hips and letting his hands run over her shapely thighs and calves, bare and warm. Then he took another rolled towel, a smaller one made of soft velour, and placed it exactly in the middle of the one that was spread over the chaise. "Sit on that."

She did, back to him, holding herself up with outstretched arms, clinging to the end of the chaise with both hands.

"I'm going to turn up the vibration. I want you to press your pussy into the towel and ride. Then I'll spank you some more." His voice was rough and shaky. Ruth sighed, giving herself a few preliminary rubs against the rolled velour almost absent-mindedly when the vibration increased in intensity.

His hand came down swiftly on her buttocks, shocking her into an "Oh!" of surprise. She rocked and pressed, wanting more—and Nick gave it to her. Without warning, a powerful orgasm coursed through her. She moaned, rubbing on the soft towel rolled between her legs until he grabbed her by the waist and made her bend down, clutching the far side of the chaise now and not the end, with her ass in the air and her high heels braced. He positioned his cock—she could feel the latex around it, he must have managed to put on a condom while she was having her pleasure ride—and rammed it home. He didn't give a damn about anything else but fucking her as fast as he could, holding her as tight as he could, and pulling her soft behind into his taut groin as hard as he could.

"Nick! Oh! Oh, oh, oh!"

Ruth knew she was on the verge of coming again and reached between her legs, rubbing her stimulated throbbing clit until the sensual, deep pulsing began. Her pussy clenched around him, forcing him to come too, in turbocharged shots she could feel as they pulsed out, into the condom tip. He cried out, thrust a few more times, then pulled back, one hand on her back and one hand on the thin rim of the condom.

Ruth straightened and turned around. Nick was breathing hard, eyelids closed, a fierce sweat trickling down his temples. He took one last shuddering breath and opened his eyes halfway to look at her. "Oh, Ruthie. Great shoes. And anytime you want to do that . . . just let me know."

Which she did. A few hours later. He was gentler this time, not quite as crazy with lust. And when she rolled on her back, cooling her tingling ass on the smooth sheets, he'd only wanted to be on top of her. Face to face. Heart to heart. Kissing her closed eyes when she slipped over the edge into a last orgasm that made her tremble all over. And holding her close afterward for a long, long time.

3

They made it into the lobby just before six a.m., dodging the maids and the rest of the sleepy-looking staff. Then Ruth spotted Eduardo and pulled Nick behind a giant urn filled with fresh lilacs and roses.

"I don't want your poker buddy to see me, Nick," she whispered. "Do something. Distract him."

Nick shushed her and waited for his opportunity. When Eduardo turned to advise a maid who was cleaning the twenty-foot drapes with a long suction rod, they made a dash for the revolving door, alarming the brass-buttoned doorman. But at least he didn't recognize them. Nick got her around the corner, laughing breathlessly, and flagged a cab heading crosstown.

They scrambled into the back seat. Nick leaned into the open partition and spoke to the driver. "Take the FDR Drive to the Triboro Bridge and let us off at—" He specified an address that Ruth didn't recognize but it sounded like it was in Queens. The driver nodded and accelerated with a jerk that threw them both against the back seat.

Ruth sat forward and closed the scratched plexiglass panel. "Why are we going to Queens?"

"Because I left my car at a precinct there. Cooperative investigation, ongoing. I'm going to take you home. Gotta get to work, though." He planted a big smooch on her, half on her cheek and half on her mouth. "You get to sleep, you lucky heiress, you."

Ruth yawned. "I'm not exactly Paris Hilton. No bedroom video, no Guess contract, no millions. Just enough to live on, thanks to my good-for-nothing dad."

"Right. I remember."

She patted his stubbled cheek. "But you weren't really listening, lover. At least we're getting the wild sex out of the way. Maybe we can have an intelligent conversation one of these days."

Nick threw his thigh over hers. "God, I hope so. But I want more of that wild sex. We don't have to stop doing that."

Ruth peered out the window, looking at the sunrise over the East River. The cityscape rose in dark blocks, but the pastel light of dawn made it seem almost lovely. She hummed under her breath.

"You sound happy. What's that song?"

She stopped humming and thought. "Getting to know you."

"Looking forward to that."

"Me too." She looked in her bag for a comb and lipstick, hoping to make herself look halfway presentable before they arrived at the Queens police station. Or for that matter, before she had to face the Agnellis.

Ruth had no doubt that Mrs. Agnelli had noticed Nicky Del Bianco come and go. The old lady had a mind like flypaper. The second she saw Ruth get out of Nicky's car and knew she'd spent the night out, the gossip would start. With a speed that beat the fastest Internet connection modems down.

Oh, well, Ruth thought philosophically. At least the bingo

players in the dismal basement of the parish house would have something to talk about besides their last trip to Atlantic City.

"So are you going to introduce me to your colleagues?"

"Sure. Why not?"

"And you're going to suggest that I work undercover, right?"

His expression got serious but he had to know that she was joking. "Of course not. It takes more than sunglasses and a distracting get-up to fool the smart crooks. And the stupid ones can't shoot straight. Either way you wouldn't want to be in the line of fire."

Ruth sighed and crossed her legs at the ankle, wiggling her toes inside the uncomfortable stilettos.

"I'm going to have those shoes framed." He captured her chin for a long, tender, lascivious kiss.

The next thing Ruth knew, the driver was waving his EZ pass, which was supposed to be attached to his visor but wasn't, at the Triboro Bridge tollbooth sensor. They bumped over to the right lanes, heading for Queens. The morning rush was already starting on the inbound side to Manhattan, commuting zombies staring straight ahead.

"God, I don't envy those people. But I'll have to go back to work eventually. Poetry is not going to pay my rent.' Ruth realized that she had let numerous projects languish since the day Nick had come into her life. She just didn't feel like doing something as tedious as writing. "Maybe I'll join the force," she said playfully. "Whaddya think, Nick? Should I be a cop?"

He shook his head. "Never works. One per family."

His mention of taking her to meet his pasta-preparing mother flashed across her mind. "We're not a family," she said carefully. "We're not even officially connected. We're seeing each other. That's all."

He gave her a long look. "But I want more than that, babe. A lot more."

Three months later . . .

The stickiness of a New York summer was setting in too soon. Ruth pushed her long hair out of her face and tried to concentrate on the words swimming on the screen.

Creativity was the pits. The screenwriting class she'd signed up for at NYU was interesting, but she didn't know how to get all the characters she had in mind into one room, let alone talking to each other. Whoever came up with that old adage—write what you know—didn't spend hours every day with a yarping mutt for company. With Nick embroiled in some huge, hairy investigation he wouldn't talk about, it was her and Tuff against the world again.

If he wanted more from here, he hadn't said what. Yeah, he called often, even sent flowers, but he hadn't been able to get away for a night for weeks. Mrs. Agnelli had even given up dusting the figurines on her windowsill and watching for his car.

Ruth turned to look down at Tuff, who banged his tail on the floor.

"Say something. Anything."

Tuff yarped.

"I can't put that in. C'mon, let's go for a walk." A word he always understood.

She grabbed his coiled leash, attached it to his collar and unlocked the front door. A blast of muggy air wilted her but she marched bravely out. Tuff didn't mind the heat so long as a trip to the World's Most Fascinating Hedge was planned. A little white female poodle had moved onto that street and she peed on the Hedge too. Tuff stopped in his tracks whenever he happened upon her scent, refusing to budge.

Ruth decided to go the other way, around the opposite corner. A few blocks of tug-of-war with Tuff would be good exercise, although she couldn't exactly call it walking.

A huge trailer truck blocked half the street ahead, and a milling crowd was gathered around it. She spotted the head-mikes on the assistants before she got there and heard the usually insufferably self-important instructions to the onlookers as she walked up. A film crew.

Tuff strained at his leash, eager to make new friend and maybe score a sandwich from the catering table set up outside the trailer. Neighborhood types were goggling at the star on the door of another trailer, whispering about who might be inside. Ruth bumped into a young guy with a multipocketed vest and a clipboard who seemed to be more or less in charge of guarding the perimeter.

"Ma'am," he began. Ruth froze. The muggy day must be making her look old or something. Her first *ma'am*. She hated him for it. "You can't walk through here, ma'am. We're shooting."

"I live just down the street. Don't tell me where I can walk."

He waved the clipboard at the action behind him. About the only breeze going on this hot day, Ruth thought irritably. "Sorry, ma'am." He steered her to one side as other crew guys went past with light stands and sound equipment. She noted the logo on the trailer truck: CB3. Despite her bad mood, which was entirely the fault of Nicky Del Bianco, who had left her unloved and unlaid for far too long, Ruth was curious.

"So what are you shooting?"

"The pilot episode for *The Goombah Girls*. CB3 Productions wants to cash in on the popularity of mob shows."

Tuff made a faint gagging sound and Ruth gave him a little more leash. But she wanted to gag too.

"Mix *The Gilmore Girls* and *The Sopranos*, and you get the idea. Brilliant, huh?"

Ruth only shrugged. She didn't think so but millions of TV watchers would probably love it.

"So we came out here to shoot an authentic Italian-American

blue-collar location. Little brick houses. Awnings on every window. White gravel in the yards and maybe a statue of St. Francis. Or those plaster Madonnas with fake roses. You know, super tacky."

She didn't like the neighborhood she'd grown up in being described as tacky. And those Madonna statues meant something to the old Italians who shrinkwrapped them every winter and set out new plastic roses in front of them in the spring. And as far as St. Francis, he meant a lot to the squirrels, who ate the birdseed and bread crusts scattered at his humble concrete feet. Not like the animals had a catering truck, she thought with indignation, wishing she could think of a way to put this kid in his place.

The guy turned around as if a sixth sense warned him that someone was important was approaching. "Whoops, the AD. Our assistant director," he added officiously. "Hey, Gil."

Gil didn't bother to say hello to her, but spoke directly to Clipboard Guy. "We need people for a crowd scene. Ask some of the locals, OK?" He glanced at Ruth. "She'll do."

Ruth put her hand on her hip and favored Gil with a killer glare. He seemed to be impervious to it. "Wanna be in a movie?" he asked rudely. He seemed not to care what her answer would be.

She was about to give him and Clip a piece of her mind, a really self-righteous piece, but she thought it over.

Why not? her shameless side inquired. *Have some fun. Nick's been crazy busy and there's nothing you can do about it. No point sitting around a stuffy apartment in the Bronx wishing he was doing you.*

"Okay," she said. Tuff tugged at his leash, reminding her of his existence and burning need to get going. "Uh, what about my dog?"

The AD flipped through the script. "No dog in the scene. Dump him at home and come back in an hour. Fifty dollars a day, take it or leave it." He looked her up and down. "Think you could change your clothes? Look more like a real goombah girl?"

Ruth stiffened. Then she remembered the outfit she'd strutted around in all those weeks ago. The outfit that in some mysterious way had changed her entire life. Brought her and Nick together, in fact. Maybe it had the power to bring him back again. She could call up Sofia and borrow it one more time. What the hell.

"Sure," she chirped. "I'd be happy to betray my cultural heritage and perpetuate damaging stereotypes of Italian-Americans for fifty bucks. No problem." Ruth was sure her sarcasm would be wasted on the AD, but just thought she'd get a few licks in. She was going to do this.

As expected, the AD didn't seem to hear. "Get her a release to sign and see who else you can hustle," he told Clip.

Ruth watched them go back into the crowd, then turned and headed home. Tuff ran ahead but stopped short suddenly, sniffing the air. "If you think that pretty little poodle is waiting around for you to show up, think again, Tuff. I bet she has better things to do."

Sofia made it over to Ruth's place in less than seven minutes. She bustled through the door that Ruth held open, carrying drycleaned clothes swathed in thin, clear plastic bags that were sticking to her legs. "Ugh. It's so muggy. I hate summers in New York. But kiss kiss, baby. We're gonna make you a star!"

"Sofia, they need extras. All I have to do is stand there. Not a chance of stardom."

"You never know. The leading lady could sprain her ankle and you'd have to go on in her place. This could be your big break, Ruthie."

She took the heaps of clothes from her cousin's arms and dropped them on the sofa. "I'm not an actress."

"You signed up for that screenwriting course. Same thing or next door to it. Whatever, it's all good."

Ruth sighed, looking for the black leather microsuit she'd worn. "Yeah? If Nicky showed up once in a while, it would be even better."

Sofia looked at her curiously. "Don't tell me he's losing interest so soon. Not when I just forgave you for landing him, even though I am married and would have to regretfully say no should he ask me."

"He's been busy."

Her cousin patted her hand. "Could be the truth. Busy doesn't always mean unfaithful. Usually it does, though."

"Thanks for cheering me up."

"Aw, c'mon, Ruth, you're gonna have a great time today. Forget about Nicky for now. Hey, d'ya think they'd want me too? I'd love to be a goombah girl. Let's have some fun. What else is there in life?"

Bambino cheeped and sidled toward them on the perch inside his now-not-so-new cage.

"See. The parakeet agrees. It's a sign."

Ruth shrugged, barely able to do it while she was still holding the clothes. "Then who am I to disagree?"

With Sofia's help, they got dolled up in less than half an hour, and decided to take her air-conditioned Caddy to go the few blocks back so their makeup wouldn't melt. On her way out Sofia glanced at Mr. And Mrs. Agnelli, stretched out flat on plastic-webbed lounges in the shady part of their driveway, trying to catch a nonexistent breeze.

"They look like a display at Rizzo's Funeral Home," she said to Ruth as she slid behind the wheel. Mrs. Agnelli lifted a hand in limp farewell and Sofia waved back. "Rest in peace," she added sotto voce.

* * *

Back on the fringes of the production setup, Clip waved them into a parking space. Apparently the black, late-model Cadillac made all the difference, because he didn't recognize Ruth right away. She pulled down her sunglasses and batted her eyes. "Remember me? I was walking my dog."

"Oh—yeah. Of course." He gaped at Sofia, whose outfit was even more gapeworthy than Ruth's. "And you are?"

Ruth noticed that he didn't call her cousin ma'am. "She's with me."

He flipped through the sheaf of papers on his clipboard and pulled out two form releases allowing footage with them in it to be used by CB3, and indicated where they should sign.

"My autograph?" Sofia beamed, and signed the release in gorgeous, flowing Catholic high school script. The last of the penmanship nuns had taught it to her. Ruth, five years younger, hadn't had that advantage. Her signature was no more than a scrawl.

Clip took the two forms without looking at them, and then pulled out what Ruth recognized as a shooting script. He flipped through to the center and said, "Take a look at this."

Sofia read over his right shoulder and Ruth, over his left, before the two exchanged a glance.

"I just want you to understand your motivation in this scene before we start rolling," Clip went on. "It's a critical moment, juxtaposing the human desire for intimacy with the bleak reality of existence."

"I thought this movie was about goombahs," Sofia said.

"I thought this was a cable TV show," Ruth said. "The AD didn't mention intimate desire or bleak reality."

Clip nodded patiently. "But it's in there. I know because I wrote it."

Ruth saw Sofia's plucked and penciled eyebrows rise. "You wrote it?" she asked. "But you're, uh—Clipboard Guy. Sorry. I don't know your name. In my mind, you're Clip."

He smiled shyly. "I like that. Kinda like Gadge. Very old school. Very film."

Sofia looked to Ruth for confirmation that Clip was actually speaking English. Ruth thought for a minute, then understanding dawned. "Gadge—oh right. Short for gadget. Gadge was Elia Kazan's nickname," she said to her baffled cousin. "He directed *On the Waterfront*."

"Ohmigawddddddddd," Sofia breathed. "With Marlon Brando. Do you know him, Clip?"

"Marlon Brando's dead," he pointed out.

"I mean this Gadge person."

"He's dead too."

"Even so. I'm impressed." Sofia looked at Clip with awe and he blushed.

The AD came running up. "Let's go, girls. We're rolling in five. I need you on the set."

"Whaddya want me to do?" Sofia said, grabbing Ruth by the hand and following him. He looked back at her. "You're taller," he said to Sofia. "Come with me. You—" He took by the shoulder and planted her by a gaggle of goombahs who were standing by, joking with the lighting guys. "You wait here. You're not in this shot."

Sofia was propelled into the crowd scene and barely had time to turn around and mouth *sorry* at Ruth. So much for stardom, Ruth thought sourly.

One of the watching guys, a skinny one, switched the stumpy cigar in the side of his mouth to the other side of his mouth and gave her a reptilian smile. "Come here often?"

"No." She edged away.

He took that as a challenge and moved in. "You're cute."

Ruth folded her arms over her chest. Bad move. She was already sweating in the black leather outfit, even though the shirt was microscopically short. She supposed she would have to talk to him. The AD hadn't said where or when she would be needed, and she wasn't going to slink away and let Sofia get all the glory.

"Thanks," she said flatly, pushing her sunglasses up her sweaty nose. "So . . . are you an extra or an actor?"

He laughed in a gurgly way. "None of the above. I'm a producer."

But you look like a goombah. She didn't say it, just looked at him.

"We got a lotta money in this production," he added. "It's my job to see that it's spent."

"Really," she said noncommittally.

"Uh-huh. Hey, you must be an actress." He sidled closer, looking around like he wanted everyone to see he was talking to her. "You know what? I got a pool. A big pool. You should come over for a swim. It's a hot day."

Okay, this was weird. He was talking like he was somebody important but he was very clearly . . . a goombah. He might even be the most dangerous variant of the species: a crazy goombah.

"Not today," she said carefully.

The AD came rushing back before he could ask what color her bikini was. He brought her to stand next to Sofia, who was fidgeting in front of a huge camera on a dolly and the bored-looking crew surrounding it.

"Follow my cues," he barked at the two women. He turned to pick up a hand signal from the cameraman and shouted. "Speed! Slate it. This is take fifteen, *The Goombah Girls.*" A guy with an honest-to-God clapboard, just like in the real movies, rushed up and clapped it front of the camera lens.

"Have you figured out what this is all about?" Ruth hissed at Sofia.

"Cut! We're losing the light," the AD shouted. A cloud drifted over the brilliant sun. Other clouds were moving in sluggishly and the heavy air felt like rain was on the way.

The crew swarmed around the camera and adjusted this ring

and that knob. Clip wormed his way through the onlookers and stood next to the AD, making notes on the script.

"I have no idea," Sofia whispered to Ruth. "They seem to be making it up as they go along."

The hubbub around the camera ceased and the AD issued the same odd commands. "Act sexy," he said to Sofia and Ruth. Her cousin pouted, flipped her hair and blew kisses at the camera.

Ruth just stood there, wondering what the hell she was going to do. If she was supposed to be wanton, she wouldn't. That was her private side, part of a game she liked to play with Nick. Not with an amateur film crew and a bunch of freaky goombahs who called themselves producers.

The black-clad men were hooting at Sofia, making obscene suggestions in Calabrian dialect. She told them what they could do to themselves in modern Italian.

Speaking of Nick . . . someone who looked an awful lot like him was easing his way into the back row of watching men. But it was hard to tell. The guy in the back was wearing a baseball cap and sunglasses. And there were other guys with him, who didn't look like they were part of the film crew either.

Something her mother had once said came back to her. *When you're in love, you think you see your lover everywhere. Or at least you see his car.*

Was that Nick? What the hell was he doing on this shoot? Well, come to think of it, he did live around here and not all that far away, near the Grand Concourse. Had he been gone so long that she'd forgotten what he looked like?

Ruth's red lips parted as she puffed out a breath, thinking. The cameraman swung her way and the focus puller made the lens zoom in on her mouth. The Nick lookalike mouthed the words *shut up* as she stared intently at him, but not before Ruth whispered, "Nicky Del Bianco, is that you?"

Clip consulted his script. "There is no Nicky Del Bianco in this scene."

"A lotta things ain't in this scene," the biggest of the goombahs said. "Like excitement. Like tits. Write in some tits, kid. And don't give me that existentialist crap."

Clip shook his head. "She didn't sign a release for a nude scene. And I'd have to get her picture with a valid state or federal government ID for a tit shot."

The goombah only growled.

"We have to prove she's over eighteen," Clip explained.

C'mon, Ruth wanted to say. *You called me ma'am. You know damn well I'm over eighteen.* But like the clouds piling up in the summer sky, the mood on the CB3 set was turning ugly. The onlookers were walking off in twos and threes, disillusioned with showbiz, complaining about not being able to park. The star still had not appeared from his or her dressing trailer, if there was a star. The goombahs were muttering to each other, meaty hands thrust in their pockets, talking about going to Mario's on Arthur Avenue for insalata de mare, a dish in which squid got respect.

Ruth searched the crowd for the man who looked like Nick. She spotted the nondescript baseball cap jammed on his head—and when he turned his back to her, she finally saw that dark-gold hair. Yeah, that was him. Those shoulders. That cocky walk.

Hot, tired, sweaty, bored, and sure, really sure that was him, she left the set before the AD could stop her. "Hey, we're not done with you!" he shouted. "Where do you think you're going?"

"Fuck off," Ruth explained.

"Cut!"

She walked up to Nick and tapped him on the shoulder. "Hey. What are you doing here?"

He whirled around and almost replied, then clamped his

mouth shut. The AD caught up with Ruth and grabbed her roughly by the upper arm. "Get the hell back on the set or I'll—"

One powerful uppercut punch from Nick took care of the rest of that sentence. The AD folded up and lay down on the sidewalk peacefully enough, eyes closed. The first few drops of rain splattered down on his face. He opened his eyes . . . and witnessed the mass exodus of the mob guys, who were crashing through hedges, getting into double-parked cars, running down the streets. The skinny one, the one who'd talked to Ruth and the last one to figure out that the so-called film shoot was turning into a round-up, tripped over the AD, who moaned. Skinny didn't even bother to get up, just stretched out his wrists for the cuffs to come.

Nick obliged, leaving the mob guy for his colleagues, done with the dirty work. "Hey, honey. Why am I here? Just doing my job. You almost blew my cover. But I still love you."

"What?"

"I said I love you." He planted a kiss on her lipsticky mouth and came up for air in about a minute, looking like a clown. "Mind if I ask you the same question? What are you doing here?"

"I can't believe I didn't figure out that they weren't legit," Sofia complained.

Nicky raised his hand, like he could tell her why she hadn't but he was too polite, so he wouldn't.

Sofia didn't figure that out either, just kept throwing the clothes she'd brought over to Ruth's apartment willy-nilly into garbage bags to protect them from the pouring rain outside. Nick and Ruth cuddled on the sofa.

"Aww. Look at the lovebirds," Sofia said. "Enjoy yourselves. I'm going home." She threw the last bag onto the pile. But run it by me one more time, Nicky. I hafta explain what happened and I don't want Joe calling here for details when you two are all hugged up."

Nick took his arm off Ruth's shoulders and leaned forward, clasping his hands. "I've been investigating mob money laundering. I'm not going to go into the details, because the investigation isn't over yet. But the production you stumbled into was fake."

"But CB3 is a real network," Sofia said. Her glittering dreams of stardom were dying down to ashes.

He shook his head. "Small outfit, using public access airtime. They own two cameras, rent studio space and hire freelancers by the day. Plus Clip. A film school student who thought he was getting a shot at the big time. I understand he was planning to take the footage to Sundance, see if he could cut a deal with indie producers to distribute it."

"Poor Clip," Ruthie said softly. "Is he going to be locked up?"

"Nah."

"Lock him up anyway. He called me ma'am."

"No law against that," Nick said, laughing. "But I feel your pain."

"Ruthie, shut up," Sofia whined. "I wanna hear the rest."

Nick leaned back. "Anyway, CB3 made a deal with the Queens branch of the Fabrizi family. They pretend to make a movie, a mountain of money gets funneled through CB3 to mob-run businesses, like a restaurant catering company and a trailer-truck company, the goodfellas play kissyface with wanna-be actresses and everybody's happy."

Sofia found her handbag. "Okay, I can remember all that. Thanks, Nicky. See ya, Ruthie." She grabbed the handles of the full-to-bursting bags and Nick got up to help her get them to her car in the rain.

A few minutes later he came back in, drenched to the skin.

He pulled off his sweatshirt and tossed it to one side, then shook the water out of his hair.

"Can't wait to see the *Post* headlines tomorrow," Ruth said. "My hero."

"Damn right."

"What are we going to do now? I'm ready for a nap. Rainy days always make me sleepy."

He stood over her and pulled her to her feet. "It's starting to thunder. That means we can make some noise."

"About time." She reached down into his jeans and found what she'd been missing. "While I'm holding this," she said, "tell me again what you said when I walked up to you."

"Are you wearing your lucky panties?"

Ruth shook her head and held his cock tighter. "As a matter of fact, I am, but that wasn't it."

"You mean when I said I loved you?"

"Yeah. Say it again."

He eased out of her grip and swept her up in his arms. "I love you. Do you love me?"

"I think I do."

He kissed her nose. "Then let's get naked."

Unzipped

1

Pam heard the sliding door of the delivery van bang open and went to the window to see if it was him. Yup. Those were his shoulders. And his dark brown hair. Even from three stories up, Kev Donnell looked good. He wore his usual uniform of delivery company shirt and summertime shorts, scuffed suede lace-ups, and thick socks that bunched around his ankles. The muscle in those legs just didn't quit. Pam watched him swing down from the driver's side and feed the parking meter, then stride around to the back of the van, unlatching the clasp.

He came around again with a white cardboard box in his arms that was almost as long as he was tall, carrying it lightly. The mystery package that he said was for her when he'd called five minutes ago. Long-stemmed roses?

Interesting. Maybe she had a secret admirer. Ha ha.

She tried to lift the window a little higher so she could call to him but it was stuck shut. Humidity. Everything swelled in June.

Kev took the stairs two at a time and disappeared into the vestibule of her apartment building. Pam buzzed him through the downstairs door before he pressed her button, knowing he'd come all the way up without waiting for an OK. Working at home meant you got to know your delivery guy.

Her accounting business was doing all right. Her clients, creative types and minor celebrities who had not one clue about how to manage their money even though they were making plenty of it, let her figure out their seriously screwed-up finances and quarterly taxes. Rather than maintain an office, she had them send in their paperwork in bulk: bank statements, usually marked up with baffled questions about why one check or another had bounced, endless credit card bills that testified to an over-the-top social life, and mountains of crumpled receipts that bore the circular imprints of wineglasses and coffee cups.

None of which arrived in pristine white boxes. Not what Kev was bringing up. She went to the door when she heard him thunder up the last flight of stairs and opened it before he knocked.

"Hiya, Pam. Package for you, as promised." He held it out, holding it at either end with strong, long-fingered hands, but she didn't take it, only looked at the shipping label.

"From Stacks, huh?" She knew the name from one of her clients, who liked to give his girlfriend ultra-expensive, super-sexy evening gowns, which she, a temperamental Russian model, liked to rip up, just to show him who was boss. "That's a dress company. I didn't order a dress." She hitched up her baggy gray sweatpants.

Kev winked. "Bet you'd look good in one."

"Aw, shucks. Bet you say that to all the slobs."

"Only the beautiful slobs like you."

"Thanks a lot," Pam said. She cast a glance into the hallway mirror by the apartment door, just in case there was a grain of truth in his friendly compliment. No surprises there: blond hair with thick bangs that needed trimming. Round eyes, bluish. Full lips, glossed, but otherwise no makeup. Pretty good boobs

and small waist, concealed under a beige sweatshirt with a peel-
ing logo that said *Can We Get Our Hands On Your Bottom
Line?*

A relic of her brilliant career at Cooper & Freundlich, ac-
countants to the stars. Playing switcheroo games with their
celebrity clients' millions got Ernie Cooper five in a federal
playpen. Lou Freundlich got off a little easier with an ankle
bracelet and sixteen months of house arrest.

Kudos for the uninvolved: Pam Kendricks got a pat on the
head from the judge who praised her honesty.

"I'm being honest," Kev said nonchalantly. "Hey, I've been
delivering here for over a year. We're friends, right?"

"Sure are," Pam said. Had it been that long since Cooper &
Freundlich had gone under and she'd struck out on her own?
"Which is why you've never seen me in anything but sweats.
Take me as I am."

Kev looked her up and down with an amiable leer. "I like to
be comfortable myself."

Pam glanced down at his mostly bare legs. Amen to that.
And how good it felt to be looked up and down in sweatpants
that didn't do anything to advertise her curves. She could count
on Kev to cheer her up.

"At least you get to run around all day," she pointed out as
she walked with him into the kitchen. "I get to sit and do taxes
for crazy people."

He slid the long box onto her kitchen table, bumping a big
wooden bowl that usually held bananas, occupied at the moment by a comatose cat.

"Sorry, Frisky."

"His name is Lump. For obvious reasons."

"Oh, yeah. I forgot." He scratched lightly between the cat's
ears. The Lump raised his head and gave a huge, tongue-curling
yawn, then went back to kitty dreamland.

"So c'mon," Kev said. "Open the box. Your name's on it."

Pam shook her head. "Is this your way of living vicariously?"

"Yeah, I get curious. And you don't ever get anything but padded mailers filled with tax stuff, so I'm even more curious."

"But I didn't order anything from Stacks. There has to be a mistake."

"Maybe it's a surprise, Pam," he said patiently. "Could be a gift. Is it your birthday?"

Birthdays. Pam loathed birthdays. Annual reminders of the march of time and the downward pull of gravity. She didn't celebrate hers and no one outside of her immediate family knew when her birthday was. And it was weeks away. Anyway, no one in her family would send her something from Stacks.

"No," she said finally. "But I'll open the box if it'll make you happy. You'll probably have to take it back, though."

He took a delivery-guy thingy off his belt and scanned the bar code on the shipping label with it. "No problem."

Pam stuck a fingernail into the thin tape that sealed the box and ran it lengthwise. "Wouldn't want to use a box cutter. Don't have one anyway, come to think of it."

The top flaps separated and she could see tissue paper underneath, folded neatly over a red something and adorned with a gold Stacks label.

Kev stuck the thingy back onto his belt and looked inside the box, interested.

"Drum roll, please," she intoned. He obliged, beating the table on the side. The cat, startled into offended life, uncurled himself from the banana bowl, and jumped off the table onto the floor with a thud, waving his tail.

Pam lifted a big piece of the tissue paper, crumpled it into a ball and tossed it on the floor in front of her cat. Lump ignored her attempt to placate him and stalked off.

She parted the rest, revealing a voluptuous heap of what appeared to be shirred red velvet.

"Wow," said Kev. "Nicer than I thought."

Pam stopped what she was doing and looked at him. "You haven't seen it yet. Did you know what was in here?"

He held up his hands. "I confess. There was a Stacks catalog with it. I compared the product code on the shipping label and so—yeah, I did know."

Pam touched the velvet without removing the dress. "I've seen that catalog. It's so unreal. Like Neiman Marcus. For people who can drop $10,000 on an impulse buy. You know, gem-encrusted pet dishes and stuff like that."

Her cat sauntered back into the kitchen with a now-you're-talking look on his face. He jumped up on the table again and stuck a paw into the box, patting the velvet.

"Quit it, Lumpkin," Pam said, shooing him away. "This is not your new nest. I won't be able to return this thing if you get cat hair all over it." She felt inside the tissue for a gift card or an invoice. Nothing.

"Hold it up," Kev said eagerly. "Let's see what it looks like."

Pam only shrugged. "Not as if I'm going to wear it." But she reached into the box, found the straps, and lifted it out of the enfolding tissue. She held it against herself, striking a glamor-puss pose. Kev's eyes lit up.

"Wow. Fantastic. You have to try it on. Red has got to be a great color on you."

"Think so? Mostly I wear boring old beige." She looked down, taking in the details of the dress. Spaghetti straps. A fitted, very lowcut bodice carefully designed to give boobs a lift without the wearer needing a bra. Subtle shirring down the front seam and bias-cut side panels that flared over the hips without clinging. It really was a movie star's dress, like nothing Pam had ever seen. She didn't want to let go of it.

"You know, I think you're right about the red. To hell with beige. My sofa is beige. My life is beige."

"You need some excitement," was all he said. His voice was lower and kinda rough around the edges.

Still holding it against her body, she walked over to the hall-way mirror and inspected herself, blowing her bangs out of her eyes with an upward puff. She caught Kev looking at her pouted lips and smiled at him.

"You said it all, Kev. Wow is right."

He kept his distance but his gaze was riveted to her, almost as if she were really wearing it.

Pam turned this way and that, marveling silently at how alive the dress seemed and feeling a flash of chagrin at how shabby her sweats looked. She didn't have to wear them every day—they were just there in the morning, easy to pull on without a second thought. Undemanding. Able to accommodate a few extra pounds without her even knowing she'd gained a little weight.

She looked in the mirror once more. And she looked at the man standing behind her. Keeping his hands on his hips made Kev's shoulders look larger and his waist leaner. His wide-apart stance was totally male and his long, strong legs were well worth a sneaky look down. Not to mention what was between them.

"Okay," Pam said offhandedly. "I'll try it on. Labels and all. Prepare to be dazzled, humble deliveryman. Have a seat."

Kev nodded, and pulled a chair out with a hasty scrape against the floor. He sat down and leaned back against the table, gently scratching Lump's head again. The cat got into it, rubbing its whiskery cheeks against his fingers for an added-value petting experience. "Ready for the show, pal? I am. Even if she did call me a humble deliveryman."

Pam laughed and headed down the hall to the bathroom, shutting the door behind her. She hung the dress on a high hook and stripped quickly, kicking the ugly beige and gray sweats and the balled-up socks she'd had on into a corner. Her practical white briefs joined the pile next.

Naked, fluffing her pubic curls, she looked at the dress one last time. Then she took it off the hook, positioned it over her head and let it slide down her body. Just putting it on was erotic. It fit like a . . . body glove. And speaking of, wouldn't it be nice if she had a pair of long gloves to accessorize it with. Diamond earrings, too. Mink eyelashes. And a gigolo on each arm.

She stepped up onto the edge of the bathtub to see more of herself in the mirror over the sink. Wow wow wow. What it did for her boobs and her butt was nothing short of amazing.

Pam stepped down carefully, inspecting her face critically. A little eye pencil wouldn't hurt. Just a dab of powder blush—but only a dab. The red velvet made her fair skin glow. When she got done with the makeup, she grabbed a brush and did a major fluff on the hair. Good to go. Then she scrabbled in a little basket of cosmetics that she hadn't used in way too long, finding a lipstick in an identical shade of red to the dress.

Pam uncapped the tube, parted her lips and put it on with precision. The result was overwhelmingly sensual. She blew herself a kiss, gave her bangs a final fluff with the brush, and opened the bathroom door.

"Don't be shy," Kev called.

"It doesn't fit," she called back, smiling to herself. Might as well play him.

"Awww." He sounded utterly disappointed.

Barefoot, Pam walked down the hall. Under the flared sides, her thighs brushed together in a way that was sensually stimulating. And the dress cupped her ass almost like . . . a man's hands. She thought of Kev's strong hands holding the box and the eager look on his face when he'd asked her to open it. Pam took a deep breath and stepped into the kitchen.

Kev almost fell off his chair. He rocked back, righted himself, and stood up. "You look—so beautiful."

"Think so?" Pam asked innocently. She strolled around the kitchen, flipping the skirt with one hand and running the other through her hair. That lifted her bosom even higher, and Kev looked hungrily at her breasts.

"Yeah. I do."

"So . . ." she breathed. "How much time do you have left on the meter?"

"What?" Kev just gaped at her.

Pam threw him a flirty look designed to melt delivery-dude belts. Maybe it was the magic of the dazzling dress, maybe it was the months she'd gone without a date, maybe it was Kevin's friendly but totally male vibe and all that healthy energy he radiated . . . but she had suddenly decided to seduce him.

No second-guessing herself. No filling out *Glamour* quizzes on whether he was Mr. Right or just Mr. Right Now. No calling a girlfriend and discussing it in advance. Her inner vixen was in charge, and inner vixens did not think twice, especially when she was pretty sure there were condoms in the nightstand drawer.

He could always go and get some if not.

Kev was just so fucking cute. The sudden admiration that glowed in his brown, dark-lashed eyes was enough to turn her on, big time, but it wasn't as if she had never noticed how gorgeous Kev Donnell was. She had just been too busy to do anything about it, what with getting a home-based business off to a solid start and donning baggy sweats every damn day to work nonstop.

But opening that white box with a flick of her fingernail changed everything. She still had no idea where it had come from or who had sent it to her by mistake, but she didn't care. If a magic dress got dropped on your doorstep, you couldn't say no. Pam ran her hands over her velvety hips. "I said, is there time on the meter?" She ran her hands up and lightly cupped her breasts. Kev clenched the back of the chair for support.

"Guh," was all he said. "Go. I mean, I'll go see." He thrust a hand into his pocket, not taking his eyes off her as he rushed for the door, jingling the coins in it and, she suspected, forcing his erection down.

Pam nodded, giving him a glistening red, come-back-soon smile. Kev focused on that for a split second, stopped, then grinned in response. "I don't believe this."

Pam murmured a barely audible, "Believe it," then picked up the cat and tickled him under the chin. Lump stretched out his neck, purring blissfully as she rubbed the sensitive spot with long strokes in one direction, completely focused on the animal's pleasure. Kev took in the sight, then ran through the open door, not shutting it behind him.

"Guess what, Lumpkin," she cooed. "I'm going to get laid. And you're going to get locked in the living room. Is that okay with you?"

The uncomprehending cat seemed to agree. He was a fool for a good chin rub. Pam carried him down the hall to the living room, grateful for once that the rooms in her ancient apartment building had doors that opened into the halls, awkward as the arrangement was. She didn't want Lump pouncing on Kev's ass once he got naked and got on top of her.

Cooing to the cat, giving him one last head scratch, she set him down inside the living room and closed the door. Then she walked back to the kitchen, hearing Kev thunder up the stairs and almost colliding with him when he burst back in.

"Easy. Calm down," she said, patting his chest. He was breathing hard.

"Fed the meter. So—this is for real, right? You want me to jump you—believe me, I want to—oh, Jesus, Pam. I thought you'd like the dress, but not this much."

She looked at him wide-eyed. "You mean you bought it for me?"

"No." Unable to resist touching her, he ran his hands over her shoulders and down her bare arms. "It's a long story. Tell you later, okay?"

"Tell me now."

His hands moved around her waist. "I just wanted to give you something. But I didn't know if you'd like the dress."

"I like the dress." She put her arms around his neck, not quite believing what he was saying but loving his confusion and his arousal.

"You're so sexy, Pam. Even in those goddamn sweats. Last few months, I couldn't stop thinking about you."

"That's sweet," she said softly. Feeling wanton and womanly, she pressed her body ever so subtly against his, as if the dress had possessed her. Until she'd slid it on over her bare body, Pam did not do wanton things, did not think of herself as a temptress, and did not, as a rule, coo. Kev's hands held her tighter, keeping her exactly where she was and not letting her get a millimeter closer.

"So, uh, anyway, I was talking to a sales associate at Stacks because I deliver there sometimes, and she happened to have the catalog at the page with the dress and I—"

Pam put a finger over his lips. "I get the idea. Kiss me."

His sensual mouth opened and then . . . he didn't do anything. "Good as you look," he began nervously, still holding her around the waist, "and I do mean good enough to eat—can you lose the lipstick? I can't finish my route with smooch marks all over my face, grinning like a fool."

"I like that picture," Pam said, smiling and letting her hips move a little from side to side. Kev drew in his breath and let it out very slowly. His body reacted. If she wanted to, she could reach a hand right under his shorts and touch his brief-clad balls. Or did he wear boxers? There was only one way to find out.

She kept one arm around his neck and moved the other one,

stroking the lightly furred front of his thigh and sliding it up to just under the hem of his shorts. Boxers. Light and soft.

Imagining pulling them down and seeing his big cock jut out made her instantly hot. But she withdrew her hand and patted his face. "Sure. No problem." Pam went to the sink and got a paper towel, getting most of the lipstick off, then running another paper towel under the hot water and blotting her mouth with it. Between the removed lipstick and the rubbing her mouth was tender. She turned to him but Kev covered the distance between them in two big steps, pulling her into his arms and kissing her with a raw, turbocharged hunger. His hands ran over her hips and behind, feeling her there with passionate intensity. "No panties, huh? All right."

He backed her up against the kitchen counter and kissed her again, a little more gently this time, exploring her mouth with his tongue and nipping her lower lip. One big hand pushed her blond hair out of the way and he moved to her neck, planting small kisses on the sensitive skin there, going down and then up again to take a sexy little munch on her earlobe.

Good thing she didn't have diamond earrings on, Pam thought dreamily. God, he could do this to her forever and she wouldn't mind.

He pulled back, looking down at her with fierce desire. "Okay, hot stuff. There's another part of you I want to taste. Ready for it?"

Without waiting for an answer, Kev lifted her up and set her on the counter, settling her butt on the red velvet so her skin didn't touch the counter but pushing the front of the dress up. He clasped her ankles and spread her bare legs. Pam braced herself on her hands and leaned back, watching him grab a chair and set it where he wanted it, right in front of her. He sat down and looked at her pussy for a long, satisfying moment. Not touching. Just looking.

Pam relaxed, feeling giddy, happy to be so shameless, so in

the moment. She knew from the way he kissed that he would treat her pussy with just the same delicious mix of mostly tenderness and a bit of roughness. Looking at his mouth, the slight smile that curved it, and the sensuality of his downcast look heightened the anticipation of the sexual pleasure to come.

When he began to stroke the soft skin on the inside of her thighs, still enjoying his intimate look at her, not glancing up, Pam closed her eyes. She could just feel his breath on her pussy, warm and soft, but not that close. She knew he was observing her body's involuntary arousal, getting off on looking at her labia, swollen and slick, turning a deep pink. His strong, caressing hands warmed her thighs and kept her from trembling.

But Kev still didn't touch or lick her pussy, just kept stroking. Then he moved his hand to the skin under her navel, stroking her there in a sensual semicircle that made her arch and push her pussy closer to his face. He dropped a kiss on the springy curls but kept his hand where it was, pushing against her womanly belly with a rhythm that she guessed was natural to him—and how he would fuck her when he got around to that.

For now, she was too into what he was doing to move. The waiting between his caresses only intensified the sensation of his hands moving over her flesh—then watching him look his fill at the succulent pussy he'd wanted for so long—both were erotic to the max.

Kev took his sweet time about loving her, and he did it right.

He scooted forward in the chair and rested his head on her thigh. Just close enough to dart out his tongue and flick it over her swollen little clit.

Pam dropped her head back and moaned, wriggling her buttocks an inch or so closer. Kev grabbed her thighs and buried his face in her pussy, licking her labia, and sucking her clit into his mouth as gently as if it were a nipple. Bingo, she thought. Oh, Jesus. This was better than anything. He slid a finger into her juicy pussy while he kept sucking clit and held it there.

She could feel herself begin to pulse around his finger and a few seconds later, Kev took his mouth away. He rested his head on her thigh again, just breathing on her clit, letting her sexual excitement subside. A move, Pam knew, that would only make her come harder.

That seemed to be something he wanted to have happen. He didn't say a word but the skillful way he handled her made her smile inwardly, wondering without jealousy what woman had taught him that.

Probably an older one. He must have been a willing student and he had obviously paid worshipful attention to his much more experienced lover.

The thought of Kev as a strapping eighteen-year-old, naked and stiff-cocked, spurting a little cum that he couldn't control, made Pam shiver with sexual excitement. She could imagine him kneeling between the legs of a woman who was as wild for him then as Pam was right now, licking his first lover tentatively, then with sensual boldness.

Sitting in front of her as he was, fully dressed, only made the fantasy that much more vivid. Pam moaned and messed up his thick hair with careless strokes, supporting herself with just one hand as he began to push his tongue between her labia, spreading them open to get deeper inside. His tongue was as long and as strong as the rest of him, and it felt a lot like a cock.

She imagined him again as a neophyte, and what he had looked like from behind, ass up and muscular thighs bunched up as he went down between a woman's legs, his balls tight to his lean body and his buttocks shaking from trying to control his imminent ejaculation. Another woman floated into Pam's fantasy, also older than the youthful Kev, one who reached between his legs to stroke his balls and reached around to clasp his hugely erect young cock with an oiled hand, pumping him until he sprayed helplessly, moaning against the pussy of the woman he was pleasuring with his mouth.

Pam gasped and pushed Kev's head away. Even though he was staying away from her clit while he licked, her visualizing a trio like that was just too intense.

"What?" he said softly, wiping his mouth. He stood up and put his hands on either side of her, kissing the creamy skin of her breasts, pleasurably compressed by the fitted bodice of the red velvet dress. "Hmm," he murmured. "I've been neglecting these." He pulled out one breast and then the other, resting them on the soft upper edge of the bodice so they overflowed it and the nipples stuck out. "Hot. I love the way your tits look like that. Really stacked. Ready to be sucked too."

But he kissed her mouth first, fondling her breasts and pinching her nipples. He tugged a little harder at them when he broke the kiss, pushing her tits together and getting his tongue into her cleavage.

Pam began to sweat. He licked up every drop. "Sexy. You taste so good. Sweet here"—he stuck a finger into her pussy—"and salty here." He licked between her breasts again but he didn't take his finger out.

She shifted on the counter, pressing her thighs around his chest. With one swift move, Kev picked her up, getting an arm under her ass and supporting her upper body with the other one.

She clung to him, not caring about the tangled dress, not caring about anything but enjoying herself with a hot guy in this abandoned way. His nice, neat deliveryman shirt was going to smell like pussy but she couldn't help that. He'd wanted to pick her up, let her squeeze him with her thighs to help him carry her—for a lusty guy like Kev, a pussy print was probably a badge of honor.

With her arms twined around his neck, he toted her down the hall. "Which way to heaven?" He kicked open the partially closed door to the bedroom when she breathed, "That way," in his ear.

Kev set her down on the bed with a bounce and didn't waste any time getting his boots off. "Gotta love speed laces." He grinned at her and set the boots aside. Then he flicked his belt open and shoved down his shorts and boxers. Just as she'd imagined it, his cock sprang out from thick, dark, curling hair. He got his balls where he wanted them with a fast motion but he was too aroused for them to hang down.

Later for that, Pam thought with pleasure. She planned to cup them after he shot his load, enjoy their spent softness—but by the looks of him now, the condom tip was going to be full to bursting with his cum.

"Dress on or off?" she asked softly.

He stood by the bed, towering over her, one hand just brushing the outside of his thigh and one resting loosely on his lean hip. The pose made him look like a Greek statue of an athlete in his physical prime.

But oh God, was he alive. The veins in his cock pulsed as he looked at her sprawled on the bed, and it bobbed a little, then got stiffer, rising smack up against his tautly muscled belly. He took himself in hand, stroking his cock to the tip, watching her watch him do it. Pam couldn't take her eyes off that mesmerizing sight. Watching men masturbate in front of her was a really strong turn-on.

She knew she could never handle a cock quite the way a man did his own—they were often a little rougher than she would be, paused to rest when she wouldn't know they had to, and could squeeze the shaft just right to hold back on ejaculating—or to make it spurt in long streams, showing off, coming with fierce male pride. And the way a man touched his own balls, strong fingers cradling both while the other hand jacked off his hot cock—that just did her in.

Pam loved to have a man come on her body: on her breasts, or straddling her waist to give her a pearly necklace, or on top of her, rubbing on her belly until he ejaculated; or even thrusting between her clasped thighs while she lay on her back or on her front, pounding her until he exploded wetly all over the sheets beneath.

But right now . . . she didn't know what Kev wanted her to do. He had amazing self-control, that was clear.

"Dress on," he said at last. "Tits out and on display. And get on all fours."

"Yes, sir," she said mockingly, but she was willing to play along. Kev going alpha was intriguing. Her pussy began to pulse again as she flipped over to get on her hands and knees. The dress slid down over her bare ass and she reached around to lift it up again.

He stopped her with one big hand. "Let me have the pleasure of pulling it up."

Pam looked up at him through her mussed hair, smiling. "All right."

Before he did that, he sat down on the edge of the bed, fondling her tits, filling his hands with them, even slapping them lightly just for the hell of it. Pam relished the way he did it, enjoyed the feel of her breasts bumping and swaying, and his hands brushing over the sensitized, sucked nipples as he slapped and fondled them gently. To be on all fours for amorous tit play felt very natural and deeply female. Having her bottom bared while he did it would feel even better—a touch of submissiveness always got her more excited than she wanted to admit.

But he had asked for that pleasure and she wasn't going to deny it to him, not in so many words. All the same, she could use her body to let him know that she was ready for that too. Pam wriggled her velvet-draped haunches and pushed against his side.

Kev chuckled a little and increased his stimulating slaps. "Want me to do that to your ass?" he murmured.

"Maybe," she said softly, not looking him in the eye.

"I think you should put on some panties," he said. "Just so I can pull them down after I lift up your dress. Pretty ones."

Pam rose up and sat back on her haunches. Kev seized the opportunity to suckle her nipples and kiss her breasts. She pulled the red velvet dress down a little and straightened the twisted middle, then got up, so turned on that she stumbled a little. She went to her dresser and opened the bottom drawer, bending way over. "I keep the pretty panties in here. Don't wear them often. Hey, these even match." She pulled out a pair made of red stretch lace. "Skimpy enough for you?" She waved them at Kev.

His hard-on got harder. "Put 'em on," he growled.

Pam flipped up the skirt of the dress and swathed the material around her middle, leaning back against the dresser to hold it there and balance herself. She leaned forward, letting her breasts spill out, stepping a little awkwardly into the stretchy panties she held spread between her fingers, pulling them up over her calves and thighs with deliberate slowness. He watched her intently. She let the dress fall back down and walked to him.

Kev grabbed her hips when she reached the bed and pressed kiss after kiss against her pussy, hidden by the dress. "I don't know which is more sexy," he said in a low voice. "Seeing it or not seeing it."

"Up to you, lover. I think I need to have you take charge for a little while. You know what I want." She stroked his hair as he looked up at her for a few seconds, then rested his cheek on the beautiful dress that made her feel so feminine and so desired.

"All fours is what I want." He gave her a slap on the butt. "Do it. But keep yourself covered."

Pam eased down, giving in to his unspoken request for a long, hot kiss on the way to the next stage. Then he put her away from him, letting her get on hands and knees, waiting for him to lift her dress.

He kneeled behind her, sliding the sensuously soft fabric over the backs of her thighs, lifting the dress inch by inch until she felt the material slide up and over her lace-clad buttocks. Kev draped it around her waist, then began to pull down her panties.

She could hear him breathing hard and his stiff cock bumped against the back of her legs now and then. He stopped when the stretchy panties were rolled down to just below her ass cheeks and her behind was bared.

He touched the lace in between her legs. "Nice and slow gets you hot. Your panties are wet. Good girl. Now get your legs farther apart but keep your ass up."

She moved her knees and did exactly what he said. Kev pulled her panties down to the middle of her thighs. The stretchy lace was taut and she got her knees even farther apart, until the elastic strained to the snapping point. She could imagine how the sight turned him on. Dress up, panties down, her round ass, big and bare, and a very, very hot pussy completely available to his fingers, his tongue, and his huge cock.

She'd had the first two . . . she craved the last.

"I think you need your pussy pounded," he said. His voice was harder now. "No more foreplay. Time for heavy fucking."

"Yes," she breathed. She felt him behind her, heard the rip of a condom packet and the slight sound of him rolling it on. Then he kneeled behind her, placing the head of his sheathed cock directly against her labia.

Pam wriggled, wanting to thrust backward. But she reminded herself, dazed with lust though she was, that he was in charge.

He reminded her too . . . by bringing both of his hands down on her buttocks for a double smack. Pam moaned with pleasure. "Uh-huh. You like to bare your ass and be disciplined a little, don't you?"

"Yes," she whispered. The feeling of being just barely penetrated by the tip of his huge cock made her want to cry out for more. Allowing him to spank her while he maintained his strong self-control was unbelievably exciting.

"Reach around," he told her. "I want you to keep your panties pulled down and your face in the pillows."

Again Pam did as he said, going deeper into the sensual excitement of the moment, aware that her half-dressed, half-naked show was making him crazy with desire. She grabbed the rolled-down elastic that kept the panties stretched between her thighs and held it with her thumbs, knowing that he was going to spank her some more.

He did. She moaned and shoved her ass up, wanting still more. He gave her that too, then rested his big hands on her tingling behind, gasping for breath, pushing his cock tip in just a little further.

"Fuck me now," she begged.

With a ragged breath, he rammed his big rod all the way up her pussy and grabbed her around her hips, pulling her back to him. His balls brushed her pulled-down panties, which she pulled up tight around the bottom of her ass before letting go, freeing her hands so she could brace herself against Kev's vigorous thrusts.

He slammed into her, crying out softly. "Feels so good—so good. Deep inside you—so hot. Make me come with your tight pussy, Pam—oh—yeah! Make me come!"

They rocked together on the bed, aware of nothing more than the heat of each other's bodies and an excitement that went so deep they truly did become one. He curved his powerful body over hers, keeping himself up on one arm and reaching between her legs to do her clit. She screamed with pleasure, writhing uncontrollably at the moment of climax as his body shook and he came too, shouting out her name.

2

Pam awoke naked, feeling a very gentle breeze move over her skin. She vaguely remembered Kev unzipping the dress and easing her out of it, letting the folds of red velvet fall into a puddle on the floor. Where was it now?

She looked around drowsily and saw it on the back of her bedroom door, on a hanger. The rich material caught the golden light of early afternoon coming through the blinds and the dress almost glowed, especially since every other color in the room was on the bland side. Kev had been right about her needing some excitement and he had sure as hell provided it.

But never mind the dress. Where was he?

She listened and heard him moving around in the bathroom down the hall, and also heard the plaintive meow of Lump, hoping to be let out of the living room so he could (a) get a snack and (b) go back to sleep in the banana bowl.

Kev must have heard him too. She heard him walk softly down the hall barefoot and turn the creaky knob of the living room door. The Lump shot out, stopped, and wound himself around Kev's ankles, judging by the nice-kitty murmurs Kev was making. Very faintly, she heard the cat purr and then Kev headed back to her. He came through the bedroom door, a towel knotted around his lean hips, freshly showered, his hair wet and spiky. Pam felt a rush of affection for him and reached out a hand to draw him down to her.

"And how are you?" Kev grinned and sat on the edge of the bed, the towel coming apart to show his cock and balls, nice and clean and damp, and smelling like her soap. She cupped it all, liking the resting softness of male flesh, and looked up at him, still a little sleepy.

"Just fine, thank you. That was fun. Sure beat reviewing 1099s and quarterly tax forms. I have to let you interrupt me more often."

He rose for a second to pull off the towel, and sat back down next to her. Pam looked him over, feeling awfully lucky. Bare-assed and gorgeous, Kev Donnell was just all around amazing. He scruffed the towel over his wet hair. "I had a good excuse, remember?" He pointed to the dress hanging on the back of the door. "Or maybe I should call it a bribe."

Pam sat up too, feeling very comfortable being naked with him. "Kev, you didn't buy that dress, did you? Stacks is a really expensive store."

"Um, no. I tried to explain that, but your mind was on other things. I sorta borrowed it. On a trial basis. To see if you would like it."

She patted his cheek, feeling a slight scratch of stubble and liking that too. No way would any man in his right mind use a razor a woman had used on her legs. "I did like it. But I'd guess it cost, what, five thousand?"

He shrugged and let the damp towel fall into his lap. "In that neighborhood, yeah."

Pam planted a big smooch on his cheek. "You're totally sweet. But you have to return it." She looked at the red dress again, feeling a flash of guilt that she hadn't asked that question before she'd let him make love to her wearing it.

She bounded up from the bed and went to the bedroom door, carefully inspecting the dress for any signs of wild sex.

"What are you doing?"

Pam raised the skirt, looking inside for stains and finding none. "A Monica Lewinsky check."

"I already did. The dress is like new. I was careful. I mean, we could have it drycleaned but then I'd have to take the tag off."

She looked for the discreet little tag that she'd tucked down the side before she'd strutted her stuff. There it was. The price wasn't on it but they couldn't return it without that.

"You could keep it," he offered. "I'll find a way to pay for it."

"Nothing doing," she said. "That's, what, two month's salary for you? We could get something like it at a discount store or Sym's, and do whatever we wanted in it."

"I liked the idea of giving you the real thing," he said, a stubborn set to his chin.

She shook her head and let the dress fall from her hands into voluptuous folds. "If you can't deduct it, why bother?" She stroked the material almost lovingly, though, noticing that the June humidity had taken care of every possible wrinkle. It did indeed look like new.

"You're way too practical."

Pam took the few steps between her and the bed and pushed her great, big, naked, gorgeous pal flat on his back. "Not all the time." She straddled him, then caught a whiff of her unwashed body, waving it away with one hand. "Whew! I have to shower. You're too clean to mess up."

Kev grabbed her ass. "I like that smell. You and me. Male and female. Hot and juicy."

She laughed. "A little too juicy at the moment." She got off him awkwardly and swabbed his belly with the damp towel. "You don't want to go around smelling like a happy pussy the rest of the day, do you? Don't you have to finish your route?" Another thought occurred to her. "Oh, Jesus—your van. They tow around here. What about the meter?"

"Took care of it. I didn't sleep very long. You were out cold, though."

She put her hands on her hips and glared at him. "Were you watching me sleep? Did I drool on the pillow?"

Kev grinned in a lopsided way. "Yes and no."

"I know I drooled."

"Not on me."

She picked up a pillow and looked at it. Nothing on that either. "Hmm. Guess you're telling the truth. I won't have to hit you with this." She did anyway, connecting with a soft whomp. Kev grabbed the pillow, pulling it out of her hand as he rose to enfold her in a hug.

"Not going to say uncle. And I do have to finish my route. Wanna ride along?"

Pam pondered that. Whatever she had been doing before he showed up with the dress in a box, she couldn't remember. So it could wait. But her practical, accountanty side reasserted itself. "Isn't that against company rules or something? I don't want to get you in trouble."

He hugged her again. "I won't tell if you won't. Not like I'm going to let you bounce around in the back of a van. Sit up front and wear your seatbelt, that's good enough for me." With his hands on her shoulders, he set her back from him. "Hey, you know what? I have a uniform change in the back somewhere. Wanna dress up again? That way, if another driver sees me, he'll think you're a trainee or something."

"Pam Kendricks, delivery girl?" She thought it over for a few seconds, then nodded. "Sure. Why not."

He squeezed her bare butt. "Into the shower. Let's get going."

Two hours later, the day was winding down. The sticky weather made her sweat but the uniform shirt and shorts were loose on her and that helped. Pam leaned forward a little in the seat to turn up the airconditioning, for what it was worth. Kev had to get in and out of the van so often it almost didn't matter.

She got to be in charge of the clipboard, making neat notations on routine deliveries all over town, doing a fair job of faking his handwriting. He made a left turn into a service road, letting the wheel spin back between his big hands, then wrestling a monster of a clutch to get up to speed again.

Pam didn't have much to do but look at him, and think about . . . well, wow. He'd gone from friendly delivery guy to lover man in the space of a few short hours. She wasn't quite sure how the hell that had happened, but she was more than happy to stay on the ride, however long it lasted.

Just looking at him turned her on—and made her heart beat faster too. As in r-o-m-a-n-c-e fast. Kev Donnell seemed to be pretty much everything she'd ever wanted in a man, she thought uneasily.

So either he would screw up or she would, sooner or later, she told herself. Pam didn't trust the word romance, something she felt compelled to spell just to take the emotional charge out of it, let alone the experience of romance.

Love didn't add up. Numbers added up. She decided to run some in her head to distract herself from dangerous thought processes that led to overindulgence in premium ice cream and fantasies of happily-ever-afters. Just watching his muscular thighs as he shifted in and out, pressing one big boot on the clutch pedal, was enough to make her want to watch forever.

An unsecured box shot forward into the well between the

front seats, and a few more toppled down. "I'll get 'em when you stop," she said. Kev went through a green light and pulled over, patting her butt as she bent over to go into the back. A nice old grandpa shuffling by saw him do it and gave Kev a be-spectacled wink and a thumbs-up. Kev grinned back, looking a little sheepish.

"Straighten up, Pammy," he said out of the side of his mouth. "Don't get the senior citizens too excited."

"Then get your hand off my ass."

Pam stacked the boxes, noting that the fallen-down ones were unwrapped toys in store boxes and not delivery cartons. "What are these? I mean, I can see that they're toys, but where are they going?"

"Here and there. I collect them from different stores, mean-ing I ask for donations, and I add a few I buy. A friend who works for a charity handles the distribution. Just something I like to do."

"Why? If you don't mind my asking."

Kev rested his hands on the wheel and looked out at the street. "Long story short, I was dropping off overstock at a thrift store and I walked in on this argument between the regis-ter clerk and a customer. They were screaming at each other in Spanish and I figured that the clerk thought she was stealing."

Pam just nodded, letting him get the details straight in his mind before he continued. "Anyway, the customer had a kid with her, a little boy, and he'd picked out a toy, a wind-up thing that bounced. Only the packaging was torn and someone'd stuck a little sign on it. *Doesn't Bounce.* That pissed me off— not the sign, that some people give broken toys to charity. So I went into the drugstore next door and bought the kid some-thing new. He was thrilled, it stopped the argument, and I de-cided to keep on doing it."

"You're one of the last of the good guys."

Kev only shrugged. "I try."

Pam stacked the toy boxes with extra care and fastened a webbed strap around them. "How am I doing?"

"You're doing great. Want a new job?"

"Nah. I actually like working at home. But I'm having fun today. Thanks for bringing me along."

Kev was preoccupied, having declared his intention to get the last of the boxes stashed in the van delivered before the end of his run. He hummed along to a heavy metal CD—Pam didn't know it was possible to hum to heavy metal but he seemed to be doing it—and he looked at her now and then with a smile that got to her emotions in a big, big way.

She smiled back—her best businesslike one—and tucked a fresh sheet of paper under the metal clip, about to mentally list the good things about him and assign each a percent value to write down. Kev didn't have to know what she was doing.

First and foremost he was a nice guy, she thought. A really, really nice guy. She wrote down 50% at the top of the page. Hot in bed. Another 50%. Pam sighed. He was already up to 100% on her improvised man-o-meter ranking and she had barely begun.

Okay. She would bend the math.

He liked animals, was kind to The Lump. 25%. Collected new toys for kids who didn't have any. 50%. Looked good wet. 30%. Pam couldn't say why that was important to her but it was. She tapped the point of her pencil on the paper, absorbed in what she was doing.

She thought some more. Able to unzip a sleepy woman and get an expensive dress off her without ripping it. 25%. Then it occurred to her that he might have practiced that smooth move on someone else, maybe more than one someone else, and she downgraded that rank to 5%.

Funny. Smart. Sweet. 35%. 35%. 35%. Healthy. Athletic. 25%. 25%. Took stairs two at a time. 15%. Tall. Pam hesitated. That was genetic and not something he'd done. But even so. 10%. Majorly hung. She smiled inwardly and gave him a solid 25% on that.

Sexy. Outrageously sexy. 50%.

"What are you doing?"

"Um, crunching numbers."

He patted her thigh and slid his hand higher, giving her an affectionate crotch squeeze. "Crunch on. We're almost there."

Pam looked around. The tall buildings radiated the heat of the long summer day and shafts of sunlight thrust between them. She could see the converted loft with the Stacks sign and get a look at the new window displays. Stacks set trends and their bizarre windows usually got reviewed on the arts page.

Blue mannequins, unclothed except for fetish underwear, were doing unspeakable things to each other. A group of fanny-packed, chino-pantsed suburbanites, refugees from a double-decker bus tour of the city, were giggling and taking pictures of each other in front of the windows.

Kev laughed at the sight and turned into the alley behind the loft. Pam looked into the back of the van for the long white box. She'd rewrapped the dress in the tissue before they'd left her apartment, checking it carefully for stains one last time. None. More magic? She couldn't say, but the dress was pristine, as if she had never worn it.

When he parked, she reached for the box, waiting until he got down to hand it to him. "What are you going to say?"

He grinned wolfishly. "That I fucked you silly in it."

"No, really."

"That it didn't fit. No biggie. I think it was a sample, actually. They're not going to sell it if it was."

"Oh. Well, then, I don't feel guilty."

He slid the driver's side door open and got out, turning to

put his foot up on the running board and take the box from her. He balanced it on his knee. "Nothing to feel guilty about. You in this dress, being as wicked as you wanted to be—I'll never forget it. Although you look just as good in my shirt and shorts."

"Aw, shucks. Thanks."

He gave her a serious look. "I mean it. The dress made you look like a goddess, but that's because you are a goddess."

"Not in sweat pants, I'm not. You're totally sweet but get real." She pointed a pencil at the box. "Bring it back."

He picked the box up again in one swing, and disappeared into the loading dock area, leaving her alone in the van. Pam leaned back and looked down at the column of meaningless numbers. So far, Kev Donnell had captured about—um—465% of something. The popular vote. As in the instant attention of every woman he who walked by him and appreciated the easy way he hoisted heavy boxes and his long strides and—lots of things. She'd seen him getting not-so-subtle onceovers all day long. What else had he captured? *Your heart*, a little voice said.

Uh-oh. She started a separate column for his bad qualities but couldn't think of any. Of course, their relationship until now had been casually friendly, everybody on their best behavior and so forth. Delivery guys had to be friendly, it was part of their job. And she bet Kev got hit on all the time. Pam chewed absently on the eraser end of the pencil, not caring that it tasted terrible.

He came back, hopped into his seat, and slammed the sliding door shut. "Nice girl. All she said was no problem, happy to help, blah blah. It's back on the sample rack and no one even knows it was gone."

Pam felt a small pang of regret. Not like she could ever wear the red velvet dress anywhere but it would be a great souvenir of the sex that had rocked her world. For all she knew, she might never have sex that good without it.

Do not obsess, she told herself sternly. Do not assign magical powers to an inanimate object. If Kev Donnell wants you, he wants you. Didn't he just say you look great in a delivery-guy uniform?

He reached toward her. Feeling the first waves of Post-Coital Nervous Second-Guessing Syndrome hit her and hit hard, she looked down at her bare thighs and pressed her knees together before he could slide his hand between her legs.

But Kev only wanted to turn her face to him, and he did, touching his lips to hers in a tender kiss that was nonetheless passionate. Purely, physically passionate.

Do not interpret this to mean more than it means, she told herself, parting her lips and yielding to the sensual mouth on hers. Tongue tango is a lot of fun. But tonight you'll be sleeping with The Lump. Kev will be heading home to—she wondered where he lived and what his place looked like and whether he had a cat or a roommate or what. She kept right on kissing him. Pam was expert at multitasking.

Kev pulled back. "Hm. Why do I have the feeling you just weren't into that?"

She scrubbed at her mouth with the back of her hand. "It was nice. I'm tired, I guess."

"Want to go home? I'm done for the day." He looked at her expectantly.

Was he waiting for an invitation? Pam hesitated before answering.

"Yeah. Gotta feed the cat, do some laundry." She realized how dreary that sounded and put a smile on her face. "Early bedtime for me. I'll make a cup of cocoa and catch a couple of cartoons on Adult Swim." Not exactly sophisticated, but then she didn't have to impress a really, really nice guy like Kev. Which was all part of his incredible charm, goddamn it.

Pam wondered what had gotten into her. Just wearing a movie star dress and being a raunchy sex goddess, demanding and receiving the ultimate in pleasure, this hadn't ruined her for ordinary life, had it? Nah.

She looked into Kev's soulful brown eyes, trying to read his mind. Despite his Average Joe job, he was anything but ordinary. Something about him made her weak inside. Made her crave more. Her ever-present common sense warned her to take it slow.

"Home," she repeated. Where she could think.

Five months later . . .

I am a woman in love, Pam thought miserably. Which totally sucks. She tossed and turned in bed, annoying Lump into jumping down and stalking off.

"Tough luck," she said to the tip of his tail before it vanished around the doorjamb with the rest of the cat. She sprawled out on the bed and punched a pillow into the right shape to hide her face and indulge in teenager-style sobs of self-pity. Feeling suffocated, she gave up on that and rolled over on her back, sprawled out even wider.

Being alone sucked even more than being in love. Kev had been assigned to a night shift at the package-sorting depot and he couldn't swing by. He was working extra hours as it was, saving up for Christmas, or so he said.

His mother wanted this, his father needed that. The nieces and nephews in his big Irish-American family adored their Uncle Kev, and he was already thinking about a small but good gift for each and every Donnell brat, as he called them. He had to be about the most generous guy she'd ever known. And he didn't have all that much to be generous with either. Her clients contributed to charities, but only because they needed the deductions.

And as far as Pam was concerned, he gave her everything she wanted. She craved his company, his easygoing sense of humor, his anything-goes attitude in the bedroom—all of him.

Her pussy throbbed with longing. Pam pressed her thighs closed. Didn't help. She thought about the new IRS regulations on bankruptcy filing and its potential impact on her business. Didn't work. She still wanted Kev, right here, in her bed, in her arms.

The phone rang and she rolled on her belly to answer it, crabbily. "Hello?"

"Hello yourself." A thrill shot through her at the sound of Kev's amused low voice.

"Hi!"

She could hear him grin. "That's better. A little enthusiasm is always nice."

"I wasn't expecting it to be you, Kev."

"Who were you expecting?"

"At this hour—I don't know. Just didn't think it would be you. How's work?"

He chuckled. "Got about an hour here between shifts, went out to my car. Just thought I'd call you. I know you haven't been laid for way too long, so I was thinking . . . how about a little phone sex?"

She drew in her breath. "You're not going to, like, do yourself in the parking lot, right?"

"No. This is just for you."

Pam unstuck her thighs. Trying to control her horniness by pressing them together wasn't a good idea. "Wow. Okay. But—um—I wouldn't know where to begin."

He laughed. "Just tell me what you want me to do to you. I'll take it from there."

"What is this, Kev Donnell's Bedtime Story Hour?"

"Something like that."

Pam relaxed and wriggled her hips into a comfortable position. Just listening to his low voice in the dark made her hot. "I want you to . . ."

"Don't be shy. Nobody's listening. You know you can tell me anything."

"I want you to come in the bedroom when I'm half asleep," she began, "and I'm naked under the covers. Then you sit down by me and put your hand on top of the covers to rub my back and my butt. I move a little but don't wake up. The smooth warm sheet slides over my skin, and it's your hand that's making it happen."

"Mm-hm."

If only he was doing that to her right now, Pam thought wistfully. Well, in a way he was, so there was no point in wishing he was actually here. Emotionally he was. He understood that she was lonely and frustrated without her having to whine about it.

"And then . . ."

"Go on."

"You concentrate on just my ass. Stroking and squeezing each cheek. Using both hands. But I'm still under the covers. What you're doing is getting me hot. I wake up a little more and you push the blankets down to my waist, keeping me cuddled up."

"You're getting me hot," he said softly, a heavy longing in his voice.

Pam smiled into the receiver. "Good."

"Now what?"

"I push up on my elbows so you can reach around and feel my tits. They're super-warm because I've been lying on my front and having you fondle them feels really good. You start tugging on my nipples and I arch up to let you. Then you start rubbing my ass with your other hand, sliding the blanket and sheets around. I love having my breasts and behind stroked at the same time."

Kev gave a long sigh and didn't say anything.

"You bend over to start kissing my bare back and push my hair aside to kiss the nape of my neck. I'm still arched up, loving what you're doing to me. Loving you."

"Do you, Pam?" he said softly.

"You know I do."

She heard him smile again. "Go on."

"Then you pull the covers all the way down and bare my ass. Tell me how soft it is and how much you want to look at me on all fours. But you take your time. You're good at that, Kev."

"Maybe too good."

"You roll me over on my back and treat me to some hard nipple sucking. I try to touch my pussy because I'm getting hot but you won't let me. You grab my wrists and keep my hands together above my head, and really do my nipples, until I almost can't stand it."

"Touch yourself now, angel. I can't stop you."

Pam's voice dropped to a whisper. "I don't want to. I'm not ready yet. I want to wait. I want you to make me wait and not rush anything. It gets really intense that way."

"Yeah."

His disembodied voice, saying that single word so softly, made her dripping wet. Pam could feel the moisture on her thighs but she kept her hands away from her swollen labia.

"You roll me back over my belly and tell me to put a pillow between my legs."

"Do it."

She shook her head, even though she knew he couldn't see her. "Not yet."

"Okay, talk about it some more."

"You want me to confide in you, tell you a really wild fantasy while you stare down at me riding that firm pillow, holding it between my thighs. I talk and talk . . . about wanting you . . . and what I do in private to satisfy myself sexually when you're not around. You tell me to go ahead and rub and lay your hands on my soft ass cheeks so you can feel me clench them . . . as I begin to lose control. Up and down. Around and down. I get to work my hot pussy and you get to watch."

"Yeah. Oh, yeah."

She breathed into the phone, imagining the size of his erection. He had to be about to break a zipper.

"Then you pull out the pillow, really fast, and take it away. I turn over, about to object, but you're ready. Your cock is out and you put it near my lips, because you know I'll open right up and suck you hard."

Kev moaned. She had him with that bit. Pam grinned and licked her lips. "So I do."

"Most of the way in. So you're comfortable."

"I press my tongue against the front of the shaft and swirl it around to under the head. And repeat that, until you have to get your fingers tightly around your cock to keep from ramming it into my mouth, you're so turned on.

"I lick your fingers too and suck you like a porn star. Hard and pulsing. You gasp and pull out, go for a condom. I lie back, pleased with myself for getting you that hot."

He didn't answer.

"Kev?"

"Still here. Losing my mind. Not touching myself. But I hope you are."

She slid a hand between her legs and kept the receiver cradled between her ear and her shoulder. "Yeah, I am. And I am so slick and tight, you wouldn't believe it. So swollen, Kev.

Waiting for you. I have my legs spread really, really wide. And I'm watching you struggle to slide a condom over your huge, stiff cock. That one breaks and you swear. I don't care, because I get to watch you do it a second time. I love to watch a man handle his cock and balls, absolutely love it."

He didn't reply.

"What are you doing right now, Kev?"

"Making a list. One item. Condoms."

"All right. You get the second one and get over me on the bed, pushing my legs even farther apart. Then you kneel and put your hot tongue where it feels best, penetrating my pussy with it. I lift my thighs up and hold myself open to get more and more. You're making me cry, it feels so good.

"Then you move your mouth a little higher and suck my clit. It's a weird feeling, almost too intense. I get my hands in your hair and make you stop. Pull you up to me so you can kiss me. So I can taste my pussy all over your mouth."

"Oh, God," he murmured.

"You can't stop now—"

"Get that thing," he interrupted her.

"What thing?"

"That dildo we had so much fun with. Put it in. I want to know that your pussy is totally filled when you start coming so you're completely satisfied. I have to go without but you don't."

"Okay. Hang on." She put down the phone receivers and looked in two of the nightstand drawers before she found it. He'd bought it in a sex shop when she dared him to go in, and like he said, they'd had a lot of fun with it, even given it a name. The Boyfriend. No matter what, he believed a woman should be pleasured in every possible place and he only had one cock.

Pam picked up the receiver. "Got it."

"Good. Lube it."

"Don't need to, Kev."

"Okay. Lie back in the pillows and hold it right outside your pussy, so you can feel the head but don't put it in. I'm over you and you're waiting to feel the first thrust."

"I want you so much, Kev. I wish you were here."

"I know. You ready, angel?"

"Uh-huh," she whimpered.

"Now. Do it."

Pam thrust the dildo she was clutching deep inside her, moaning, wishing his mouth was covering hers and moaning too.

"Yeah. I'm in you, fucking you hard but not fast. A slow thrust in with clit pressure at the end. And slow reverse while you writhe. I keep on doing it. Use the dildo just like that."

Pam lost the receiver in the sheets for a few lust-crazed minutes but she figured he would understand. She thrust the sex toy into herself, extremely stimulated knowing that he was listening to her very real moans, and had a huge hard-on he couldn't do anything about. She rolled over onto the phone and heard it beep, then grabbed it. "You still there?" she whispered.

"Yeah. Figured you lost the phone. Good. Still have that thing rammed up inside you?"

"Mm-hm." Her voice sounded far away to her own ears, shaky with unfulfilled desire.

"Hold it in and sit up on your thighs. Use the bed to keep it in. Like we changed places and I'm on the bottom and you're riding me."

Pam obeyed.

"Now rub your clit. Get the Boyfriend exactly as deep as you want it. And put the goddamn phone down."

She did but carefully, wanting him to hear her orgasm. Pam got her clit between her fingers and stroked it, increasing the pressure and speed until she was moaning again. With the big dildo deep inside her, with the sensation of Kev's presence in the dark, quiet room, she knew it wouldn't be long before she came.

Aching with longing, she touched herself just as lovingly and expertly as he did, and curled over when a powerful climax rocked her body. She pushed her pussy down on the dildo, crying out again and again, calling his name. Then she collapsed and fumbled for the phone, leaving the Boyfriend inside her throbbing flesh.

"Nice," he said softly.

"Oh, Kev. That was amazing. No matter what, you do it to me. You don't even have to be in the room."

"I wouldn't take it that far. I think I can get out of here before dawn."

"Mmm," she murmured drowsily. "I hope so."

"Go to sleep, beautiful. And when I come in, I'm going to do exactly what you just told me. Step by step. I remember every word you said." He blew a soft kiss into her ear and hung up.

3

Christmas was three weeks away and Pam was already tired. Her clients were scrambling to reduce their taxable income with year-end deductible donations and sticking money in their IRAs, at least whatever they had left to put in. For some reason, creative types, when flush with cash, tended to squander it on dubious investments: shares in Patagonian llama ranches and chicken-nugget-restaurant stocks and things like that.

After years of being an accountant, Pam had a feeling that the best way to save money was not to spend it in the first place, especially around the holidays. But she knew that Kev—sweet, generous Kev, her own personal sex god—loved Christmas and would go all out. He had dragged himself out of bed by noon, the equivalent of dawn for a night shift worker, and gone out to find the perfect tree.

Therefore, she had to find him a truly great present. But what did you give a guy who truly didn't care a whole hell of a lot about material things?

That question wasn't easily answered. She finally decided to trust fate and follow whatever called to her. So far she had been called to a deluxe athletic wear store, where she had contemplated buying state-of-the-art sneakers with innerspring soles to replace his beloved but very scuffed suede boots.

But he loved those boots.

Next, she'd gone into an audio equipment store with the interesting name of Bang & Olufsen. Apparently buying their high-end goods was supposed to be akin to a religious experience, not retail. Pam decided that God didn't want her to spend a month's salary on speakers for a guy who'd blow them out listening to heavy metal anyway.

That left something sexy. She wasn't going to wrap herself up with a bow and a tag that said ho-ho-ho, although he probably wouldn't mind. He could have her anytime, without the wrapping paper, and she didn't want him to think she was too cheap to buy an actual gift.

As to what he was giving her, Kev wasn't saying. Not dropping the most infinitesimal hint.

Pam closed the spreadsheet file on her computer when her cat strolled in front of the monitor. "Hello. You hungry again?"

He meowed. The Lump was always hungry. She had an irrational notion that he was capable of eating the bananas, peel and all, just so he could fill his furry belly and go to sleep in the bowl.

Leaving him sitting on her desk, she got up and went into the kitchen, rattling the box of cat food to get him to follow. He appeared a few seconds later, and she dropped a few crunchy bites into his dish, just for form's sake.

Then she made herself a cup of tea, cinnamon apple something that smelled vaguely Christmassy, and sat down to think. The red velvet dress came to mind. But she couldn't buy that for him when it really was for her.

And besides, he'd said it wasn't really for sale. Pam sipped her tea, letting the warmth and spicy smell clear her mind. Actually, he had been a little vague about that dress from the beginning and some of the things he'd said about it hadn't made much sense. A pricey store like Stacks wouldn't let a delivery guy walk out with an expensive dress, even if it was a sample. But maybe she should have been brave enough to buy it, even though she hadn't wanted him to blow that much on it, back when they hardly knew each other.

She finished her tea, feeling refreshed but well aware that she still didn't know what to get him for Christmas.

The sound of thundering feet in boots coming up the stairs snapped her out of her reverie. Kev was back. There was a rustly sound—pine branches—in the hall, followed by a thump as he set down the sawed-off trunk. Pam opened the door. The tree was taller than he was. Kev peered around the side, grinning. There were pine needles in his hair and pine needles stuck in the wool of his plaid jacket. "Whaddya think? Not big enough?"

"Bring it in. With the star and the base, it's going to touch the ceiling."

"All right," he said with evident satisfaction. He pinched the needles to release their cold, sharp fragrance. "Nice and fresh. Hope you like it."

"I love it. Our first Christmas. Geez. Hang on while I get the camera." She went down the hall, trying to remember where she put it.

He dragged the tree in, holding onto the trunk with a leather-gloved hand. "What for? It isn't decorated."

"I want to get a picture of you with it," she called from the living room. "All lumberjacked up and looking cute."

He stood it up when she came back, looking brawny and sexy and sweet enough to make her swallow the sentimental tears that made her a little misty. She squinted at the little digital screen and tried to get him and the tree into the frame. "Smile," was all she said.

Christmas Eve . . .

They'd visited his parents. Her parents. His brothers. Her college friends. They'd wrapped and shopped and wrapped and shopped. Pam had given in at last and gone to Stacks to see if she could find the red velvet dress. No one there even knew what she was talking about. She'd resigned herself to getting him a big, fat gift certificate to an electronics store so he could pick out the laptop he'd been talking about.

Not very imaginative, but what else could she do? A really good laptop was the best present she could come up with at the last minute, and she knew he would love it. She'd tucked a red velvet thong for her to wear into his stocking, along with a Matchbox car and candy canes.

They collapsed on the sofa and looked at the Christmas tree they'd decorated together. Kev had found about a million orna-ments in the basement of his parents' house and brought them over, carefully hanging every single one once they'd got the tree to stand up straight. She almost couldn't see the needles under the decorations. The tree sparkled richly and the big colored lights made her think of childhood Christmases, before every-one got so damn tasteful and into white wicker reindeer that nodded electronically.

Kev poured himself a shot of single malt from the very ex-pensive bottle his brother had solemnly presented to him. Pam had been pleased to see that Kev had given Doug the same thing. They did it every year. So maybe he wouldn't mind that her present for him wasn't so imaginative.

He sipped it, savoring the flavor. The Lump jumped up on the coffee table and sniffed the glass in Kev's hand, widening his golden eyes when the fumes went up his nose.

"It's whiskey, Lump. Have some. Good for your whiskers." The cat shook his head, not liking the fumes, and Kev laughed. "Look at that. He's a teetotaler." He scratched the cat between the ears and got him purring. The Lump settled down next to him as he sipped and watched Pam put back an ornament that had fallen off. "Ahh. Doesn't get any cozier than this."

"Nope." She was feeling wonderful, absolutely wonderful. Being alone with him at last and looking forward to sharing breakfast in bed with him on Christmas morning was joy, pure and simple joy.

"When do you want to open presents? Now or in the morning?" He didn't wait for an answer. "I'm a now kind of guy myself."

"And why is that not a surprise?" Pam's voice was gently teasing.

"Well, I got you something really good."

Her heart sank a little. "Oh, my."

"Go ahead." He leaned back with the shot glass in his hand and gestured to a long white box under the tree. A familiar-looking box Pam looked at it with surprise. She could swear it hadn't been there when they'd left earlier in the evening.

"That isn't . . ."

He was humming to himself, trying to look nonchalant. Much as she loved the guy, he couldn't carry a tune. Could be Metallica, could be a Christmas carol, there was no telling.

Pam crouched under the tree and pulled out the box. "You didn't."

"I did."

"You spent way too much money."

"My sales associate friend gets an employee discount. I'm not completely crazy. Except about you."

Pam was too blown away to reply. Or meet his loving gaze. She ran a fingernail down the tape that sealed the box and opened the top flaps. There was the tissue paper, neatly folded, and there was the Stacks label, gold and gleaming. And there was the red velvet dress.

"Take it out. Put it on. Christmas comes but once a year."

She left the room and came back wearing it. Kev's eyes lit up. "Yeah," he said with feeling. "Come sit in my lap." He grabbed her hand and pulled her down to him, making her laugh. The cat meowed a faint protest until Kevin turned to him. "Hey, kitty, I heard they're serving free mice in the kitchen. And three's a crowd."

Lump stayed put until Kev put a hand under him and scooped him off the sofa. The cat stalked out.

And then the fun began.

Double Dee

1

The cups were way too pointy. Not good. Dee took the proto-type bra off the figure form and set it on the design table, perch-ing on a high swivel chair to study the thing. The lightly padded, stitched nylon cups jutted up almost threateningly. She poked a finger into one, denting it. Slowly, ever so slowly, it rose again.

"It's alive," she murmured. "It's alive and it hates me."

Her assistant, Jami, came over to take a look. "What's the problem?"

Dee pulled pins out of a pincushion and stuck them through the side panels of the bra into the graphed cardboard that cov-ered the table. Then she consulted a paper pattern.

"For one thing, the design specifications are in Chinese." Dee read over the fine print. "No, this part's been translated. Sort of. Says here that the improved stitching will add a touch of el-eganceness to make this bra outstanding in all the ways."

"Um, it does stand out, Dee. A lot."

"Yeah, in the wrong way." Dee scowled and set a pair of long, heavy shears across both cups. She could almost hear the trapped air whoosh out. "I didn't ask the manufacturer to add stitching, and the Love-Lee-Lace people won't finance my new line with a prototype like this." She picked up the shears and set them aside.

Jami watched the slow, inexorable rise of the cups. "That is so creepy."

"That's what we'll call it," Dee said bitterly. "The Creepy." She ran a finger over the embroidered concentric circles of one cup. "Or the Scratchy. And how about that color? I don't think it even has a name."

Jami peered at the nylon material of the bra. "Well, it's kinda blue. With a little beige mixed in. Call it bleige. Or bluege."

"Either way, it's awful. What am I going to do? Getting to this stage of production cost me five grand so far, including the trip to China." She kicked the suitcase under the table. Thirty hours of flying backwards across who knew how many time zones and she hadn't even walked in her own door yet, coming to her rented design loft first.

Jami gasped. "Excuse me for saying so, but that does not look like a five-thousand-dollar bra."

"No, it doesn't. It looks like a five-dollar, bargain-basement nightmare." Dee plopped her head into her hands. "I blew it. And to think I talked my Uncle Isador into bankrolling me."

"I thought Is was your great-uncle."

Dee looked up, surprised that Jami would remember that little detail. "That's right. He's ninety-five."

"That's totally old," Jami said wonderingly. "He must eat healthy. But he can't live forever."

"Are you implying that he's going to die before he finds out that he sank fifteen grand into the world's ugliest bra?"

"No, Dee. I didn't mean that, you know I didn't."

Staring down at the pinned bra, Dee wiped away a tear. "What am I going to tell Uncle Is?"

"Don't tell him anything. Distract him. You could fix him

up with that fitting model who came in last month. The one with the giant boobs," Jami said helpfully.

Dee shook her head. "Silicone."

"Like men care," Jami scoffed.

Dee contemplated the hideous bra without saying anything for a few moments. "He's going to be so disappointed. He's always been incredibly kind and generous, and he believed in me when no one else did. But no one will ever buy this."

Jami hesitated before speaking again. "Well, it's not that bad," she hedged. "I mean, my grandma had a bra like that."

"Uh-huh. Now I feel better."

Her assistant pulled on a dangling thread. "I could pick out the stitches for you, but the little holes would show," Jami offered. "Maybe that would flatten the cups."

"Flat is not a concept that sells bras," Dee said. "Think round. Think high, firm, sexy. That's what sells."

"Those cups are high, Dee. And the 1950s look is hot right now. Think rocket ships, aerodynamic locomotives, ballistic missiles. You know, thrust."

"Thrust is a guy thing."

Jami studied the bra on the design table. "But my grandma's bra really worked for her. She was married three times."

A flicker of interest lightened Dee's big brown eyes. "In the same bra?"

Jami nodded. "Yup. It was her something old for all three weddings. You know, for luck. Something old, something new, something borrowed, something blue."

"Oh, that's just great," Dee said with disgust. "So I reinvented your grandmother's lucky old bra. Color me talented."

Her assistant picked up the bra and examined it closely. "It's very, um, sturdy."

"Another word that does not sell bras."

"But maybe—"

"Jami, women want their lingerie to convey sexuality, not sturdiness. It's not like army boots."

Her assistant looked down at the lace-up, khaki-colored, lug-soled clunkers on her feet. "Army boots are cool."

"Bras are different. Sexy and frivolous—that's what sells. And a good lingerie sales associate will persuade a customer to buy two or three at a time, so the ones she's not wearing can rest."

Jami looked at her wide-eyed. "I didn't know bras needed to rest."

"They don't," Dee sighed. Her assistant was just too naïve to breathe sometimes.

What Dee needed was a seasoned veteran of the fashion business with a gimlet eye for the details of garment manufacturing and the ability to crack a measuring tape like a whip. What she had was a crunchy idealist who mixed camouflage prints and pink fake fur.

Jami shook her head disapprovingly, making her eyebrow rings clink. "Designing something to fall apart—that's so cynical."

"And so profitable," Dee pointed out. "Lingerie purchases tend to be emotional anyway. Women want the illusion. It makes them feel better about themselves."

"So you're saying that a new bra is like chicken soup for the boobs."

Dee sat up straighter in her chair. "Right. We're selling hope and happiness just like everyone else." Not that this prototype would make anyone happy, but Dee had to sound confident, if only for her assistant's sake.

Seemed like an awfully long time since she'd graduated from the same fashion institute as Jami. Fashion had been fun at first but the business side of it was a lot tougher than Dee'd expected. As of yesterday, her uncelebrated birthday, she was twenty-nine and ready to quit. She looked into Jami's innocent face and saw herself once upon a time. Unbearably young. Dewy. Completely clueless. "Illusion is everything."

"Oh."

"Lingerie design is all about oo-la-la styling. A nickel's worth of satin and lace can add up to a fifty-dollar retail sale."

Jami stuck a finger under the strap of her acid-green sports bra and snapped it. "Wouldn't know. I personally like neo-urban stuff. Anyway, priced that high, a bra shouldn't spring a seam and die on you in three months."

"Tell that to the Love-Lee-Lace people."

Jami only shrugged. "They want to charge fifty bucks. But the bra my grandma got married in all three times was a Perkette and it only cost $6.95."

"Those days are over," Dee said wearily.

"History of Underwear 101." Jami paused to think. "Perkettes were the first department store bras that clicked with women. Available in white only." She looked at Dee with scholarly pride.

"Right," Dee said. "They had straps that could hoist a piano and triple-thick elastic sides with reinforced stitching." She poked the bra on the table again. "And a teeny-weeny white satin rosebud between the cups for extra allure. Just in case a man ever got that far."

Jami nodded. "They sold fifty million nationwide."

Dee leaned back in her swivel chair. "And then came La Perla," she said. "And Victoria's Secret. And Agent Provocateur. What made me think I could beat them?"

"You're a great designer," Jami said loyally. "You will."

"Not with this thing." Resolutely, Dee slid one blade of the shears under the fabric between the cups and cut them apart.

"What are you doing?"

"I think the cups are too close together. Adding a fraction of an inch in between might help. So I'm going to handsew a little extra material here"—she stuck a pin on either side of the cut— "and send it back to the manufacturer in China. And I'll tell him to take the stitching out before he starts the production run."

"Sounds like a plan," Jami said. "I'm going out for wheat-grass juice. They have minced carrot loaf on Tuesdays. Do you want some?"

"Uh, no. But thanks. I don't suppose I could ask you to pick me up a burger."

Jami shook her close-cropped head. "I don't eat anything with eyes, Dee. Please don't ask me to be an accessory to violence." She picked up her hemp shoulderbag and left the loft.

Home. Bath. Bed. The three little words that meant the most to Dee at the moment. She'd dragged the suitcase through the lobby, balancing a roll of sketches on top of it. She'd been so tired she hadn't even bothered to put them in a tube or rubber-band them. At least she hadn't left them in the taxi. She looked around for the doorman in case there were packages that had been delivered while she was in China, but he was nowhere to be seen.

The elevator door closed silently and she counted the floors going up, almost staggering down the hall to her apartment when the doors opened. Dee unlocked the door and bumped her suit-case over the threshold without bothering to turn on the lights. She stopped, letting it fall over. The sketches rolled away but she didn't bother to pick them up.

Dee shucked her clothes where she stood, then headed into the bathroom, stark naked and shivering a little. Her thighs and butt were sore from endless hours of sitting on a plane—a hot bath would take care of that. Then bed. Tomorrow was another day, although she couldn't sleep in.

Dee crouched by the tub, turning on the faucet full blast, and tossed in an extravagant handful of pricey bath crystals, a gift from a fabric supplier, so she could afford to waste them. The jar was already half empty.

The gift basket had also held a scented candle at least a foot high, lovingly created by a hive of very busy, very talented designer bees just for her, if she wanted to believe the label. She could almost see them patting it smooth with their little black paws. If bees had paws. Whatever. She had been saving the candle for a moment like this.

Dee took the basket down from the cabinet shelf and unwrapped the delicate, crinkly paper around the beeswax pillar, ready for a little atmospheric soaking. She twiddled the wick upright, then padded back to the living room, looked in the box over the fireplace for the matches, lit the candle and carried it back.

The tub was nearly brimming and Dee set the candle down on its wide ledge. She shut off the faucet and let some of the hot water go down the drain so it wouldn't overflow when she got in.

Her bathroom was her refuge—a beautifully appointed space, like the rest of the apartment. Something she couldn't possibly afford as a start-up designer, but it had been her graduation gift from Uncle Is, who owned the building. And to whom she would be in hock for the rest of her life, Dee thought unhappily.

She closed the door tight and reached into a deep cabinet for a stack of fluffy folded towels to place next to the huge tub. A bowlegged table held spritzy little bottles of beauty products and two-week-old copies of rag trade publications. Her mailbox was probably crammed with the new issues, something else she'd get to tomorrow.

She stepped in, then sat down, letting the water's penetrating heat and fragrant steam work their magic. *Ahhhh.* She leaned back, resting her head against the cool, smooth porcelain.

Bliss, just bliss. She closed her eyes. A faint, very faint, sound of footsteps echoed in her ears. Someone in the apartment downstairs was in the bathroom right below hers. As expensive as the building was, a lot of the construction costs had gone into luxury surfaces for the interiors, and it wasn't all that soundproof. She waited for the clonk of a toilet seat flipping up. She didn't hear it.

The new inhabitant of 16-B would have to flip up the seat because he was a guy. Unless he was a hardcore bachelor who never put it down. She didn't know too much about him besides his name, Tom Driscoll, noticing it on the row of mailboxes after he'd moved in three weeks ago.

And noticing him. Dee had seen the delivery van on her way out to buy a weekend's worth of fashion magazines and newspapers and thought he was one of the movers at first. Tom Driscoll's arms were massive, chest ditto. Legs, long and muscular. Dark hair, dark eyelashes. Blue eyes. Worn jeans with an eye-catching front bulge, topped by a frayed T-shirt with a few paint spots.

Never mind the moving-man clothes, she'd thought. He had to be making a lot of money to buy a place in her building. She'd scoped him on the sly, knowing he was watching the movers manhandle a ten-foot black leather sofa down the truck ramp and not her. Dee slunk away the second he'd turned toward the door with keys in hand and a big grin on his face.

Not that he would figure out that her apartment was on top of his unless she introduced herself and told him. Too bad. He was definitely the kind of guy she wanted to be on top of. Not that she had the time for a romance.

Maybe someday, she'd thought on her way back, swinging the plastic bag of magazines and munching on a Swiss chocolate bar. He'd been directing the unloading of still more black leather furniture. He had to be single and he had to be straight.

Bachelor-pad black leather stuff was the first thing a live-in girlfriend or new wife kicked to the curb, and gay guys didn't think it was cool. Not even retro cool.

Dee sank lower into the water, feeling deeply relaxed already.

She reached out with a dripping foot and turned on the hot water faucet with her toes, thinking about her China trip and the problems of the prototype. Screw that, she told herself. Think about Tom Driscoll. Think about sex.

In the habit of topping off the tub until the bath was exactly the temperature she liked, she let the hot water trickle for a few minutes. Then she heard the click of a medicine cabinet door being opened in the bathroom below. Maybe he was shaving for a late-night date. Dee could imagine what he would look like post-shower, buck naked, with wet hair that trickled water over those big shoulders. And a towel tied just above his groin, barely covering that interesting bulge.

She wouldn't mind yanking off that towel and playing with his cock and balls while he squirted gobs of aerosol shaving cream into his hand and slapped it on his face. She loved that smell, loved watching a man shave.

And she would love to kiss and nuzzle the big cock that stood up from his damp, clean pubic curls. He'd let her, of course, but when he picked up the razor, he'd tell her to quit it, giving her a sexy-Santa smile in the middle of all that white foam.

She'd let him finish. And then . . . there was nothing nicer than kissing the baby-soft cheeks of a freshly shaved man. She'd nip his neck and earlobes, and trace her fingernails over his strong chest.

Dee mentally moved the action to her own personal cloud nine, her antique fourposter. She slid a hand between her legs. If he were on all fours over her right now, with his mouth on her pussy, licking and nipping her labia and thrusting his tongue deep inside, she'd be in heaven.

Just the thought of looking up at a set of heavy balls and a thick, erect cock, her head resting between two strong thighs while he satisfied her first, aroused her to fever pitch.

Her fingertips touched her clit, brushing over the sensitive tip. Over and over. She would tease his scrotum with her own tongue, licking all around, warmly, lasciviously, feeling it tighten and his cock get thicker, wanting him to get totally hot while he serviced her but not be able to come . . .

She heard him swear and opened her eyes. Maybe he'd cut himself shaving. She looked down and realized that the water in the tub was almost over her shoulders. She sat up, screwed the faucet handle the other way, and got out gingerly, being careful not to slosh.

Dee listened for more signs of life from the apartment below but heard nothing. *Take care of that little cut, Tom. Nice to have met you. And welcome to my fantasy world.* She smiled as she wrapped a towel around herself and used another to dry her legs and arms. The first towel fell off when she wrapped yet another around her wet hair and she left that one on the floor, rubbing her wet feet in it.

Dee ran a hand over her thigh, noticing how dry her skin was. Long flights were just not good for human bodies. Her legs and ass could use some lotion. And her breasts too. Best for last. She could get close to climax with some just-right fondling and nipple attention, especially if she watched herself do it in the bathroom's tall, freestanding mirror.

Then she could finish off with a vibrator in her bedroom— the long, neon-pink Orgasmo or the small but extremely effective Ode to Joy? Decisions, decisions. Either one would do, though, and then she could fall asleep. Not a bad way to end a generally disastrous day. She put a folded towel on the ledge of the bathtub and sat on it, reaching for the lightly scented lotion, pouring a warm stream over one stretched-out leg and catching the excess in her palm, rubbing it into her skin in long strokes.

She did the same with the other leg, then stood, rubbing her oiled hands over her ass cheeks, savoring the sensual pleasure of handling herself just the way she wanted to be handled.

The steam had cleared enough for her to see her blurred reflection in the freestanding mirror at one end of the bathroom. Dee wrapped a fresh towel around her lotioned-up hips and ass, sliding it back and forth, enjoying the towel's nubby texture on her skin. She danced a little, a basic bellydance wriggle from a half-remembered class, making her heavy, firm breasts bounce. Dropping the towel, she took both her nipples in her fingertips and tugged at them. They got longer instantly and she bent forward, bare ass out and legs apart, like she was about to push her breasts into the face of a seated man.

Tom Driscoll, of course. Sitting on a chair wearing faded jeans but bare-chested. With an obvious and sizable hard-on going down one thigh.

I really like playing with my tits when you watch, Tom. But I want your mouth on my nipples. She pinched them gently, enjoying the sensation. *Sucking one and then the other. Like you can't get enough. Just looking at big, gorgeous tits makes your cock get huge.*

She grabbed the bottle of lotion, shot a stream into her palm and rubbed it over both breasts, circling the nipples, then pinching them harder. Dee closed her eyes, wanting to imagine her new downstairs neighbor more than she wanted to see herself. Her breasts would more than fill his big hands. She hadn't been nicknamed Double Dee in high school for nothing.

Now, if Tom Driscoll was watching her right now, hungry for her, going crazy from watching her caress herself, she wouldn't mind that at all. Dee cupped her breasts from underneath and squeezed them together into a deep vee.

Want me to lie down so you can put your cock between there, Tom? Nice and tight and slick and hot. I can get the pressure just right. Tit fucking can be really intense.

She imagined him over her, holding himself up with muscular arms, while he thrust and pumped between her lotioned breasts, about to spray a hot stream of cum. But she wouldn't let him. Not right away. She'd pull her breasts apart and push him off, then stand up.

Get on your knees and go down on me. I want you to lick my clit while I play with my nipples.

He'd obey, his body trembling a little from frustrated desire, and his cock gleaming from the lube, super-stiff and totally aroused. Dee would run her fingers through his hair and keep his head in place when she felt the first tentative touch of his tongue.

Give me the tip. Just flick it. Yeah . . . like that.

The condensation on the mirror had nearly cleared. She studied herself, imagining Tom Driscoll again, kneeling in front of her to eat her pussy. Her fingers got busy but she didn't want to come without the fantasy of a man doing her. Going solo was fine, but sex with a hot, thick-cocked guy was better.

She bent forward a little, her big breasts swaying, her other hand coming up to brush over the nipples. Dee began to move her hips as she masturbated, putting her whole body into it.

She began to moan under her breath, saying Tom's name in a breathy whisper just to have a man's name to say, until she orgasmed. *Unh. Unh.* Her mouth opened with a satisfied gasp. *Good one. Thanks, Tom.*

Hold on. Her eyes widened. Did she just hear a door open? And a man's voice? Dee whirled around. Caught in the act? No. The bathroom door was tightly shut.

All the same, there was someone on the other side of it. Someone who was saying, "Looks like I got here just in time."

Holy freakin' cow. What was she going to do? Throw bath crystals in his eyes? Kill him with a pillar of beeswax? Dee blew the candle out, wrapped the largest towel she could find around her body, tied it over her tits in a hasty knot and tried to remember where she'd put her haircutting scissors. Not much of a weapon but better than nothing.

Then she heard a second voice, a familiar one with a distinctive accent. The janitor. What was he doing in her apartment and more importantly . . . who was with him?

"Yes, you is right," Blastovik said. "You are in time just."

Tom Driscoll noticed the outline of light around the shut bathroom door and a faint whiff of fragrant, moist air coming from the same direction. The doorman had assured him that Dee Skinner, the tenant in the apartment above his, was on a business trip to China.

Well, if that was true, someone else was taking a bath in 17-B. And his bathroom ceiling in 16-B was about to collapse. An ominous, two-foot-wide bulge had formed and there was a steady drip from its center. There had to be a plumbing leak and he wasn't about to wait for 5,000 gallons of trapped water to bring the ceiling down.

He'd called the janitor, a morose Eastern European guy who Tom had pegged as a world-class incompetent. In exchange for doing less than nothing, Blastovik got a basement apartment and the chance to watch hours of international soccer on bootlegged cable. He said there was nothing wrong with Tom's ceiling and hung up.

After another few minutes of watching the bulge, Tom had gone down to the basement and waved a fifty-dollar bill at him, shouting over the match of the century, Bulgaria vs. Albania. Blastovik, a true fan, wouldn't budge until Tom offered to record the muddy conclusion on TiVo. So here they were.

Blastovik was clutching a can of wood putty, his remedy for everything short of thermonuclear war, and looking toward the bathroom. "Your problem, she is in there."

Astute comment, as far as it went, Tom thought. "No, she's in China."

"She is in there," Blastovik repeated, hitching up his gray, oil-stained workpants with his free hand. "The doorman says China, but he knows nothing."

Tom listened to faint sounds from the other side of the closed bathroom door. Muffled sounds that seemed to involve towels and then maybe somebody looking for something in a cluttered drawer. "Hello? Sorry to bother you but—"

The bathroom door was flung open with a bang. Tom just gaped.

There stood a goddess, clad in a towel that was just big enough to cover an amazing rack, from what Tom could see. He got the details above the neck next: pouty mouth, brown doe eyes and spiky wet eyelashes.

Oh, geez. He fell in love on the spot.

Her long, flowing hair was pinned up in a haphazard way, and she emanated a freshly scrubbed radiance and a lovely smell. A womanly, sexual smell. Tom looked over her shoulder into the bathroom to make sure she was alone.

"What are you doing in my apartment?" the goddess asked irritably. She was clutching a pair of scissors, he noticed.

Tom held up his hands. "We come in peace. Please don't stab me."

She crossed her hands over her breasts to keep the tied towel where it was but she didn't let go of the scissors. "Blastovik, what the hell is going on?"

"Miss Dee, there is a ceiling what bulges in Mr. Tom's bathroom."

"So why aren't you in his apartment?"

Blastovik pondered this question for a long moment. "He thinks you are leaking."

"I just got out of my bath and I didn't let the tub overflow. There may be a leak but it's not my leak."

"Can we look?" Tom said, trying to sound affable. She wasn't buying it. She glared at him. It was an I'm-at-the-end-of-my-rope glare, not an I-hate-your-guts glare. He hoped.

"No. I just got off a thirty-hour flight and I worked late on top of that. And my new bra is a nightmare, and you scared the crap out of me. I really don't need the aggravation."

"Oh. I'm really sorry. About your bra, I mean. And the other things," he added, feeling like an idiot.

Dee tossed her hair over her shoulder. "I'm not wearing one."

I can see that, he was about to say and didn't. What was she, cantilevered? He'd never seen breasts that big *and* that firm. And he was a breast man, all the way. Why hadn't he known that the best set he'd ever seen was living right upstairs?

She's a beautiful woman, he reminded himself. A whole person. There had to be much more to Dee Skinner than just an amazing rack. Yeah, right, another part of his anatomy retorted.

"I design bras, just in case you were about to ask." She waved the scissors at a roll of papers on the floor in front of him.

"Oh," he said. "I wasn't going to ask, but that—that would involve bras, wouldn't it? I mean the one you're not wearing." Tom winced inwardly at his attempt to be polite and sound interested. *Way to go, buddy. You sound like you have an IQ of about forty.*

She gave him a withering look. "Listen, I'm not going to stand here and chat. I have to have a new prototype ready to scan and send within twenty-four hours to a Chinese manufacturer, complete with specs and a purchase order for material."

Blastovik bent to pick up the roll of paper, straightened up, and dropped it. The first sheet unrolled from the rest. The two men stared down at a bra sketched in bold strokes of velvety red. A bra with major uplift but barely-there engineering. The kind of bra that could bring a strong man to his knees. Tom dropped to his and began to roll up the sketch, trying not to look at it. "Sorry we bothered you, Ms. Skinner."

"Give me that and get out of here." She clutched the towel

and looked at him like she really would stab him with the scissors if he didn't.

"But my ceiling—" Tom began, handing her the rolled sketch.

"I don't care about your stupid ceiling! I'm going to bed!"

"What if it collapses?" he asked the janitor.

Blastovik shrugged and tapped the can of wood putty in his hand. "She will fall down eventually. Maybe tonight, maybe tomorrow night. Maybe never."

Back in his apartment, Tom surveyed the buckling ceiling one more time. New cracks radiated out from the still dripping center but it didn't seem to be falling down. Yet.

He yanked off his T-shirt en route to his bedroom and caught a glimpse of his bare chest in a mirror. Giving in to a moment of male anxiety, Tom curled his arms under to broaden his shoulders and pump his biceps. Not bad. Then he slapped his belly, which could be called rock-hard *if* he sucked it in and *when* he hadn't overindulged in takeout Chinese food. But tonight's moo shu was showing a little.

No biggie. Seemed obvious to him that an intelligent woman like Dee wouldn't be overly impressed by gym rat abs. He sucked in his belly and struck a he-man pose, then relaxed. He looked pretty good.

Now she was close to perfection as far as he was concerned. Physically. And mentally. There was a lot going on in those doe eyes, he'd picked up on that right away. And he actually liked the way she'd thrown him and Blastovik out of her apartment.

A bra designer. How cool was that? His most favorite piece of feminine apparel was her specialty. Tom had spent his formative years mastering the manly art of getting hooks and eyes apart, and when he'd hit his teens had made out like a one-handed bandit on every date, every basement nuzzlefest, and every sporting event sponsored by Booker High.

An unbroken record of joyful unhooking that stretched back years. If you didn't count the last twelve months.

After the so-called love of his life had dumped him for a hedge fund king with a gut and a bald spot and two other girl-friends, Tom had done the curl-up-and-die thing for a while. Especially since the hedge fund king was his former boss.

But he had uncurled eventually. Collected new clients, hoovered up some available capital, and started a hedge fund of his own. The Driscoll Group wasn't in the top of *Fortune*'s rankings but it was doing nicely, thank you.

Sex had been the last thing on his mind lately, but now that he'd met Dee, it was first and foremost again . . . and making the front of his jeans twitch.

Tom looked down. His erection was straining against his fly. Good thing it hadn't decided to say hello to Dee five minutes ago. She would've kicked him and that crazy janitor down the stairs and tossed the can of wood putty after them for good measure.

He headed for the bedroom, unzipped and slid off his jeans and briefs in one go. No sense wasting a solid hard-on. Tom flopped backward on his bed, looking up at the ceiling. What-ever Dee was doing in the room above his, she wasn't making a sound.

He grabbed his stiff rod and dedicated the session to her, keeping the vision he'd seen—rosy, damp and towel-clad—in his mind. Five minutes oughta do it. Then he could sleep.

Tom rolled over onto his side, cock in hand, and checked the nightstand drawer for some glide, squirting it into his palm to warm it up. He settled back into the pillows, giving his rod an upstroke that twisted around the head lightly and then swiftly down.

Now if he could do that while she watched . . . even better. He imagined her eyes on him, half-closed and dreamy but in-tent on his hand action. She might even bend forward for a better look, flicking her tongue around the hole, lapping up the first pearly drop of cum.

Just thinking about that made a drop appear. He left it there, pumping himself with slow strokes to just under the head of his cock. Whew . . . he was getting too hot. He took his hand off and rested his head on it, letting his erection cool off a little. But it didn't go down. Thinking about Dee parting her wet, soft lips and taking him in her mouth made him stiffer than before. And if she happened to have on that red velvet bra in the sketch . . . bending over so that her amazing tits were spilling out of it . . . Tom felt a little more cum pulse out involuntarily. He rubbed around the plum-purple head, slicking himself, fantasizing about her eager tongue doing the honors, her fingers wrapped around the shaft and stroking.

He added a red velvet garter belt to his dream Dee. One that would frame her curvy ass just right, with red elastic straps that pressed into her soft flesh and made it look even softer. He wondered if she liked to be spanked. *Turn around, Dee*, he whispered in his mind. *Turn your back to me and bend over. Way, way over. Legs apart. Don't be shy. Spread and show me everything.*

Her long, dark hair had to hang almost to her waist. She'd play with it before she did what he wanted, sashaying around in that red bra and garter belt—he added stockings to the visual—then twisting her flowing hair around her hand and pulling it forward over her shoulder. Then, hands on hips, she'd bend from the waist . . . real slow. Grab her ass cheeks and squeeze 'em with red-fingernailed hands. Nice and slutty. Uh-*huh*. Then she'd pull her cheeks apart suddenly. Give him the show of his life while she cooed at him over her shoulder and talked about how much she wanted his cock in her pussy. To the hilt.

He thrust his hips up, matching the rocking to the pumping, holding himself more tightly. He hoped her pussy was au naturel, with delicate soft curls to tickle his balls when he rammed it in and pounded her from behind.

Tom squeezed his cock hard, pressing a thumb under the tip in front to keep from coming.

He wouldn't put it in her right away, he decided. No, he'd make himself wait until he'd eaten her out. From behind, with her still spreading her ass cheeks with her hands, digging her red fingernails in and moaning. His tongue would slide in and out while he put his hands over hers and helped her keep her bottom spread, and her pussy taut and stretched wide. She would love that—he couldn't really do her clit from behind but a hot tongue-fucking would be an intense warm-up for the next stage.

Dee looked like a pretty healthy girl but he could still pick her up easily, no problem. He would turn her around, sweep her off her feet and lay her back on his great, big, unmade bed. If he landed her just right, her tits would come partway out of the red velvet bra, bouncing and brimming over the uplift cups. Nipples popping out. Then she would caress her overflowing, succulent flesh—pinch the tips and beg him in a breathy voice to suck her hard—oh, jeez.

He couldn't believe how much he wanted to see her do that. And more. Hear her talk soft and low and dirty. Get her on top and let her ride, letting him reach up and cup her tits. He'd sit part way up to suck on her erect nipples while she cried out with pleasure, wanting more and more, pushing them in his mouth . . . Tom stroked himself hard and tight and superfast, shooting a pulsing stream of cum that nearly hit the ceiling. A few drops splattered back onto his tense belly as he moaned her name under his breath. As for the rest . . . okay, he would have to change the sheets. Goodnight, goddess, he thought dreamily. Sleep well. He did a fast clean-up with his gym towel and tossed it in the general direction of the laundry basket. Good enough. Tom rolled over and passed out.

Not for long.

The bathroom ceiling came down with a crash about an hour later. He half-woke, and sat up, groggily realizing what had happened, coughing a little from the dust that drifted through the air into his bedroom. He blinked at the clock.

Fuck it. Tom flopped back down into the pillows. Blastovik was useless and nothing was going to get fixed at this hour of the night. He wondered if Dee had heard the crash and imagined her coming to his rescue, still wearing only a towel. *Are you all right?* she'd ask anxiously, and then . . .

Fat chance. He remembered her saying that she'd gotten off a thirty-hour flight not all that long ago. Dee was probably out cold. He blew her a kiss, and went back to sleep.

2

Dee sipped her morning coffee, which the deli downstairs had sent up with an ancient cruller for no additional charge. The coffee was hot and black and came in a paper cup with no logo, and it was awful. But she refused to stand in line, ever, behind anyone ordering a double skim fluffacino with a squirt of hazelnut goo and an artistic dusting of cinnamon.

She liked having the time alone before Jami came in. The sun poured in the high windows of the design loft, almost blindingly bright. Dee was feeling almost human after seven hours of uninterrupted sleep. She drew on the sketch in front of her, adding side views to the red velvet bra that Tom Driscoll had gotten all stupid over.

Her private fantasy about him had been right on target. Interesting. She sketched another version of the bra with cutouts for the nipples and idly added a nice pink pair. Tom would like those. Very suckable. She heard Jami let herself in and kick the loft door shut behind her with one army boot.

"Hell-ooo," Jami yodeled. She walked over to Dee's drafting table, dropping her messenger bag and jacket on the floor along the way. "I brought you a smoothie. The Invigorator. Carrot juice, soy milk, and fresh pulverized ginger."

"Can't wait," Dee said untruthfully. "Just set it there."

Jami pulled the container out of a paper bag and put it to the side of the unrolled sketch. She took out another, flipped back the little door in the lid and took a noisy slurp of the thick green liquid inside. "Mmm. I'm having a Chloro-Phyll-Me-Up."

Dee nodded. "Sounds yummy."

Jami peered at the sketch. "Back to the old drawing board, huh? Love the red. The nipple cutouts are cool."

"Thanks." Dee thought of the man who'd inspired them and blushed but her assistant didn't seem to notice. Jami took another slurp of her smoothie.

"Want me to run over to Feingold Fabrics and get some material? We could get started on a new one. Where did that other thing go?"

Dee pulled the first prototype out of the drawer underneath her drafting table, and stretched it out. Even being rolled and stuffed in a drawer overnight didn't flatten cups like that. Slowly they rose as both women watched.

"I still think it has possibilities, Dee," Jami said thoughtfully.

Dee picked up her pencil and tapped it on the sketch. "*This* has possibilities. This is a bra that gets a reaction."

"Really? Who else has seen it?" Jami's eyes widened.

"Um, a friend."

"Oh." Jami finished the green drink by tipping the cup back and letting the last of it slide down her throat. "That was dee-lish. I'm going out to Feingold's." She tossed the empty cup in a tall wastebasket and headed for the door, kicking the jacket and messenger bag she'd brought in out of the way.

"Take some money from petty cash," Dee called after her.

"But don't spend more than five dollars a yard. Better yet, get remnants."

Jami clomped over to the diamond-quilted steel box on the filing cabinet and took out a handful of bills. "Want any trim? Sequins, ball fringe, rickrack, stuff like that?"

Dee studied the two versions of the bra, with and without nipple cutouts. "Nah. This is a little too tacky as it is."

Jami came back. "There's no such thing as too tacky. Tacky rocks."

"In your world, maybe. But I gotta impress buyers in the heartland."

Her assistant nodded her head. "Where Elvis still lives."

"Elvis didn't wear bras, Jami."

Jami waved a hand airily. "If you say so. Okay, keep it plain. But keep it red."

"I intend to," Dee grinned. The awful coffee had perked her up a little and she was ready to work. Jami was sure to come back with something interesting; she always did.

When she heard her assistant going down the stairs, she took out a fresh sheet of paper and began to draw. Not bras, just random outfits she'd seen on people in the street. And faces. Nothing like a city for providing endless inspiration. Dee sketched absent-mindedly for several minutes, covering several sheets of paper in quick succession, then lifted her pencil when she realized that she'd drawn Tom Driscoll in a half-profile. Just the line of his jaw and a suggestion of his nose. Hmm. She added his eyes. Sexy eyes. And his hair, tumbling over a strong neck.

Why stop there? She drew his shoulders. Muscular arms. A chest that showed to advantage under that all-American classic, a plain white T-shirt. She let the line continue, sketching in mighty thighs in well-worn jeans with a few swift strokes.

She added a big bulge in front. How completely yummy. Dee finished the drawing with more care, getting the jeans just right over the long calves beneath. Feet and toes—um, bare. She couldn't remember whether he had been wearing shoes or not but he had been awfully quiet in her apartment. She gave him big feet and sexy man toes to balance the mass of his body and sat back, very pleased with the sketch.

Maybe she should show it to him, Dee mused. No. She wouldn't want to give him the idea that she had been looking at him that hard or thinking about his toes. But it was a good likeness. And the other, smaller sketches of the clothes and accessories she'd noticed on the way here were worth keeping for later reference. Dee set glass weights on the drawings, and picked up the smoothie, popping the lid as she swiveled away from the table.

Carrot juice and soy milk had to be good for you. She took a sip and gagged. Maybe it was, but pulverized ginger was a little too invigorating. Dee got off her chair and went to the sink, pouring the smoothie down the drain little by little, turning on the faucet full blast to help wash it down.

It was nice of Jami to bring her breakfast and the last thing Dee wanted to do was hurt her assistant's feelings. She crumpled the empty cup and tossed it in the wastebasket, then turned off the water.

"Hated it, huh?" Jami was standing by the table, holding a plastic bag that said Feingold's.

"No. I drank some."

"Don't lie. You'll never get into heaven if you lie," Jami said.

"Dang. So whadja get?"

Jami hoisted the bag of fabric and set it on the table. Then she noticed the drawing of Tom Driscoll. "Who's that?"

Dee didn't really want to explain. "Um, a friend."

"Oh. The friend that reacted to the bra?" Jami moved the glass weights off the drawings, shuffling them until she got to the sketch of the bras. "You said it got a reaction." Humming under her breath, Jami put the drawing of Tom back on top. "He's so built. Lucky you. Where'd you meet him?"

"He lives in my building but I don't really know him. So he's not exactly a friend. I mean, I said hello to him in the lobby a couple of times. And I've seen him on the street."

"Barefoot?"

Dee picked up the bag of fabric and dumped it all out on the table, covering the drawing. "Great stuff, Jami. I like this red stretch velvet. How much did you get?"

"A yard. Feingold said we could have the whole bolt for fifty dollars."

"A yard is all I need for now. But call him and have him set the bolt aside for us."

"Okay." Jami paused and looked at Dee expectantly. "But you didn't answer my question."

"What question?"

"About your friend."

"Oh, him. Yeah, he was in my apartment last night. He lives downstairs, right under me, and he thought my pipes were leaking and the janitor let him in and yes, he was barefoot. I think. I was only wearing a towel and basically wanted him out of there as fast as possible."

Jami pushed aside the mound of material and looked at the drawing of Tom Driscoll. "Why? He's so hot."

Dee reached out and rolled him up, curling the edge of the paper over his sexy toes first and making him disappear. "C'mon, Jami. Let's get to work."

Twelve hours later, they had a bra. Dee folded it and slipped it into her tote bag, along with the other half of a takeout roast beef sandwich. Jami had averted her eyes when Dee ate the first half around six p.m., then asked to leave to get ready for a date.

Not a problem for Dee, who kept on working on the red

velvet prototype until she was pretty sure she had something. She'd said as much to Uncle Is when he'd called and he'd praised her to the skies. Old sweetie. Just talking to him made her feel better. He told her not to work too late and she promised to be home by nine, not that he would check on her.

Blasting loud music in the empty loft got her even more revved up. Of course she could design the bra of bras, which would sell in the millions! It was only a matter of time! Then she'd settled down and handsewn the pieces, not wanting to try it on when it was bristling with pins. No telling what it would look like or feel like until she actually had it on.

That she could do at home. And the Chinese manufacturer would just have to wait until tomorrow morning before she sent him the sketches and the specs.

She switched off the overheads and locked up, clattering down the loft's metal stairs to the street. A taxi swerved over at her upraised hand and she got in and got home in record time.

Once there, she changed into sweatpants and took off her bra and top, hoping the prototype would be worth the hours of labor she'd put into it. She pulled it out of her totebag and slid it around her waist, using a safety pin in place of the hook and eye closure she hadn't had time to set in.

There was a knock on the door. "Who is it?" Dee called, sliding it around to the front and flipping the cups over her breasts. She slid the straps onto her shoulders. Oomf. It squashed her. Oh, hell. Under a T-shirt this would look like a mono-boob, not two high, firm, round breasts.

"Tom Driscoll," came the reply. "The ceiling fell down."

Skip the peephole check. She recognized his voice, nice and deep. She wasn't going to have a chance to change into anything more flattering. A fallen ceiling qualified as an emergency. Good thing she hadn't gone into her bathroom, she might've gone through the floor.

She threw on a baggy T-shirt, glancing with disgust into the hall mirror as she went to open the door. She did have a mono-boob. Totally weird. Well, he wasn't going to stay and with luck he wouldn't even notice.

Dee unlatched everything and opened the door. There stood her downstairs neighbor, smiling and holding a bag from Ber-tollini's. The best Italian takeout in town—and it would beat half an old roast beef sandwich, for sure. But he looked suspiciously well-groomed in a white linen shirt worn outside of newish jeans.

"Hi, Dee. Want to share? My treat. To make up for bothering you last night."

She checked him out. God, he looked good, but she didn't have let him know that. "The ceiling fell down, huh? Where's the plaster dust? You look a little too clean."

Tom grinned. "It happened last night. The building owner is letting me stay in the penthouse apartment. I understand he's your great-uncle."

Dee opened the door wider and motioned him inside. "That's right." So that's how Tom had known she was on her way home, dinnerless. Uncle Is was not above doing a little matchmaking. "Nice guy. He suggested Bertollini's."

Dee took the bag from Tom's hand and brought it into the kitchen. He followed. "They have killer lasagna. Is loves it and it hasn't killed him yet."

"Yeah, that's what he said. I got some."

When Tom went to the kitchen window to look out, she tugged at the red velvet bra on the sly. The safety pin was uncomfortable and the way the cups squeezed together was making her a little breathless. Unless it was him.

"Hey, we have almost the same view."

Dee stopped fiddling with the bra and got busy unloading the bag. "Yeah, how about that. A brick wall. Sometimes when the light is right I pretend I can see through it to the harbor."

Tom laughed. "Your great-uncle said he was pissed when the

condos went up next door. The builders bought air rights before he could."

"Sounds like you two hit it off."

"I guess we did. Anyway, Is was in the lobby this morning and he overheard me yelling at Blastovik, so he came up to take a look. Got a team of workmen in there pronto and I can stay in the penthouse until they're finished."

"Everybody needs an Uncle Is," Dee said with feeling. She wanted to rub up against the refrigerator and adjust the latest version of the bra from hell that he had financed, but all she could do was stand super-straight to try to keep it from creeping.

Tom didn't seem to notice a thing. He kept his eyes firmly fixed above her neck, she noticed, not letting them drift downward once. He really was trying to make up for last night, even though she'd been pretty rude. Well, he had made a dumb comment about bras, but she couldn't really blame a person with testicles for doing that. Men couldn't help it.

Tom came over to the table and looked inside the bag she was unloading. "Just a thought. We could have dinner up there on the terrace. They included plastic forks and knives, and we could grab a couple of plates from your place and take them up. Want to?"

Dee managed a smile. Dinner for two on a penthouse terrace and she was wearing sweats and a sloppy T-shirt. And a mono-boob bra. "Okay." She could change . . . unless that would make him think she thought this was a date or something. Which it wasn't.

She started getting the takeout containers back in the bag—and paused for a fraction of a second when he put a hand on her waist to move her to the door. "Moon rises over the harbor in fifteen minutes. Let's go."

Dee didn't move away from his hand. She liked the strength

and warmth of it, and the way he curved his fingers around her side for just a fraction of a second until he let her go.

"Got any wine?"

"Huh? Um, yes. There's cabernet in there. And merlot." She pointed to a cupboard over the kitchen counter, enjoying seeing him stretch up for the wine and flex his muscular arms to reach the bottles.

"Which one is better?" he asked, setting down two.

Dee made a show of inspecting the labels, not really remembering. She didn't drink wine very often and the bottles had been gifts. "They're both good."

"Then let's bring both."

He had to stretch even higher to get the good wineglasses she never used. The linen shirt rose up and she caught a glimpse of muscular belly with a light trace of fur disappearing into his boxers. At least he hadn't planned everything down to the last detail. But she didn't mind how fast he moved. Considering the fantasies she'd indulged in, he could move even faster.

If Tom and Uncle Is had hit it off, that was a recommendation right there. Is checked out his buyers carefully, even though they didn't have to pass the rigorous screening of a co-op board. "I run a nice building," Is liked to say, with heavy emphasis on the nice.

Tom had the wine bottles in one hand, and two wineglasses crossed at the stem in the other. He looked like an ad for wine, in fact. Or an isn't-it-romantic ad for condoms. She remembered the way she'd imagined his hard-on straining against snug jeans as she made him suck her nipples.

"Plates?" he said pleasantly.

"Uh—of course." Dee drew in a breath and collected her wits. She got two paper plates out of the cabinet, slid them into the bag and threw in a handful of paper napkins. Bertollini's lasagne was fabulously gooey and messy, a multilayered arrangement of thick, homemade noodles, meat sauce, four different kinds of cheese, and Italian sausage. With a dash of chopped parsley on top for health reasons.

"Don't forget the corkscrew."

"Right." She rummaged around in a cutlery drawer until she found it, then stuck it in his shirt pocket, stainless-steel wings folded, curly tip up. It made the pocket sag a little but Tom didn't seem to mind. He still didn't look down, only at her face in a way that made her feel melted.

Shaking off the feeling, Dee led the way, holding the bag close to her monoboob. She stuck her feet into her red velvet Chinatown slippers before she got to the door, thinking irrationally that at least something she had on matched. The sequined dragons on the toes were about as glamorous as she was going to get tonight.

Once in the elevator, Tom pressed the PH button and leaned back against the paneling, looking at her with a calm smile. A few passengers got on and off, between floors, noting the lit penthouse button but not remarking on it.

Dee stared at the floor numbers as they passed. They had risen higher than the brick wall that shielded the apartments on the lower floors, and went higher still. She felt a little giddy. The elevator stopped with a bump and opened into a private foyer. She stepped out first, smelling the newness. Fresh paint. And a cut-wood smell that made her sneeze a little.

"The carpenters just installed the kitchen cabinets. Reclaimed teak from a Cunard ocean liner."

"Only the best for Uncle Is. He was thinking of living up here himself."

"Really? It's empty except for a few basics. Table and chairs, a sofa, and a bed. I brought up my own linens. I assume you've been here before."

Dee shook her head. "Not recently. The penthouse was finished long after the building went up and the other apartments were sold. Now Is says the pigeons make him nervous and the elevator ride makes him dizzy. I know he hasn't sold it yet."

"Interesting. I wouldn't mind living here. Big place for a single guy, though."

They walked through the apartment to the terrace, where wrought iron bistro chairs had been set on opposite sides of a small table. Dee looked over the harbor. No moon yet, but on a clear night like this it would be a spectacular view when it showed up.

She set the bag on the table and unloaded it again, grateful that there wasn't a breath of a breeze to turn the paper plates into Frisbees. Tom got to work on the bottle of cabernet, pulling out the cork with a squeaky pop that made her jump a little, and poured two glasses. She dished up the lasagna and salad, and they both sat down.

Tom raised his glass. "Behold."

As if he'd ordered it up, an enormous moon appeared just above the horizon, casting a wide band of light that shimmered around the tiny boats in the harbor far below.

Dee picked up her glass too. "That's a major moon. Let's drink to it."

They did. The first bottle was gone in no time as they talked through dinner, eating everything in the bag until the last forkful of tiramisu, carefully propelled by Tom between Dee's parted lips, disappeared.

She took the fork from his hand and licked it absent-mindedly. Dee was feeling nothing but happy. "So what was it you said you did? Run a hedge fund?"

"Mm-hm. The Driscoll Group. Doing great so far, but I'm not rolling around in money yet."

She pointed her licked fork at him. "When you do, invite me. I've always wanted to roll around in money."

"You're on." He turned his wineglass by the stem and looked at her until she felt all melty again. Dee stared down at her paper plate. It had been too long, way too long, since she'd taken time out for a date.

And this counted as a date.

"Well, you know what I do."

"It's a noble calling."

Dee giggled. "I plan to make a million. Unfortunately, my latest design is held together with a safety pin and spit, but I think I'm getting there." She covered her mouth to hold back a faint hiccup, and waited, hoping there wouldn't be more. She hated having hiccups.

Tom stared into her eyes. A beautiful, hiccup-free stillness washed over her. Wow. She had better keep talking. And a little more wine to calm her down wouldn't hurt. She poured herself another glass, and poured him one too.

"I was trying on that red velvet one you saw in the sketch just when you showed up with the Bertollini's bag. Sewed it today." That was a test. Would he keep his eyes firmly fixed on her face? He did. "You get a gold star. You didn't look down."

"I wanted to." His voice was just a little rough around the edges. So sexy. So male.

Dee's eyes went wide. "Oh. But there isn't anything to see. This thing is giving me a monoboob."

"A what?" He couldn't help smiling.

"Oh, you know. Like what a sports bra does—mash and flatten." She pulled her T-shirt up to her collarbones and leaned forward. Tom looked down at last. So did she. But the stretchy red velvet had softened and now lifted her breasts up just right, to full, creamy-skinned perfection.

"Jesus," he said, a note of awe in his voice. "Put those away."

Dee gulped and dropped her T-shirt. "They were mashed together before. I don't know what happened."

He seemed to be struggling to keep a straight face. "Hey, you just invented a magic bra, Dee."

"If I did, it only works with Italian food."

Tom cleared his throat. "Maybe that's it."

Dee blushed, embarrassed by her impulsive act but pleased all the same by the look of wonder in his eyes. "You know, this version might be The One. I have to take the seams apart and draft the pattern. If my overseas manufacturer can get it together, I might make a million after all. And then I can pay back Uncle Is."

Tom looked at her thoughtfully. "What does he have to do with it?"

"He financed the start-up of my lingerie business. Just to be nice. He's a great guy, he really is. I like him a lot better than my parents."

"Oh. And what do they do?"

"Psychologists. Mostly they argue, and it usually starts off with that classic shrink question. How-do-you-feel-about-that. The truth is, after being married for thirty years, they don't really want to know."

"Okay. That's understandable," he said slowly. "And, um, do they live in the building too?"

"No. In the Bahamas. They're both retired."

He let out his breath and poured himself another glass of wine. "Good. I don't want any members of your family to know that I just saw your breasts. Much as I liked seeing them." He drank half the glass, and coughed a little. "And I will never forget seeing them. But I think it's time I took you home."

The moon, much smaller now that it was nearly overhead, cast a bright, faintly blue light over the terrace. Dee could see his expression clearly. He was interested in her, with a capital I. Which was great, because she had sort of forgotten what it felt like to have a man look at her with that degree of sexual longing. And as soon as she had the time for some serious fooling around, Tom Driscoll would be her first choice. He was a genuinely good guy. And smart. And sexy. And even pre-approved by her beloved Uncle Is. And if Tom respected her enough not to make a move on her after she'd pulled a stunt like that, she was looking forward to their next date. What she needed right now was to go to sleep. She'd draft the bra pattern tomorrow and get it in the works. Because it most definitely, although quite unexpectedly, had worked on Tom.

"Okay," she said cheerfully. "Sorry about that. I wasn't really trying to tease you. I was just, you know, being sort of an idiot." She waved at the wine bottle, knocking it over, grabbing it, and righting it. "Cabernet does that to me."

Tom made a mental note to find another bottle. He was sure there was one in his apartment. Which was not on the way, if he was going to take her home, but maybe she would be interested in seeing his new bathroom ceiling. Then he remembered it wasn't finished yet. Maybe she would be interested in seeing where the old ceiling had been.

"So, besides the bra, what do you like about me?"

"The bra has nothing to do with it, Dee." Tom set down his glass of wine on the coffee table and looked at her hopefully.

Dee stayed at the opposite end of his black leather couch. "I'm not so sure."

"Aha. You need reassurance." He leaned back, resting his arm on the arm at his end of the sofa, and sprawled out a little. "That's why you're six feet away."

"Not my fault your couch is so big."

Tom favored her with a wicked grin. "We could meet in the middle, you know."

"That's so obvious."

"I would like to. What would you like to do?"

"I don't know." Dee did know, but for right now, she was inclined to put off the moment of truth. Indecision allowed her to breathe, something that she was finding difficult to do when Tom was so near. Six feet of scuffed black leather upholstery between them just wasn't enough. She could well imagine that

he had scooted across it dozens of times, wrapped untold numbers of women up in passionate hugs, and then had hours and
hours of fabulous sex with them. Sounded pretty good. She
squirmed closer to the arm of the sofa and stared straight ahead.

"Am I wrong in thinking that you're, ah, interested?"

"Interested in what?"

He cleared his throat. "Sex."

She coughed and took a teeny-tiny sip of wine. "Eventually.
It may be inevitable." This cabernet was really good. He'd
brought the bottle out from a different cabinet once they'd left
the terrace and returned to his apartment.

Bad move. Tom had gone all out: uncorked it with dramatic
flair, done the swirly-sniffy appreciation thing, and set the bottle on the table so she could see the label.

"Inevitable, huh?" He looked at her sideways. "Okay, I'm
staying here."

Dee sat up a little straighter. "Fine with me." Clearly he didn't
want to rush her, wasn't going to pressure her, planned to let
her set the pace. Which made her even more nervous. "Whatever.
You didn't answer my question."

"I'm thinking about it." Tom rubbed his chin, making a
faint, very faint, bristly sound.

After nine at night, he needed to shave but his stubble was
exactly right for nuzzling purposes. And Dee was definitely up
for that, and a few other things she wouldn't admit to. He just
looked too damn good in sprawly male mode and semi-ripped
jeans. Very après-work, very relaxed, very sexy. He shifted a
little, as if he needed to adjust his balls but was way too polite
to do so in front of a woman he didn't know very well. She
checked him out on the sly for a fraction of a second when he
looked away, just to make sure that . . . yes. Possibly a semi.
And long for that stage.

Tom turned his head and caught her looking at his crotch.
Dee blushed to the roots of her hair and took another teeny sip

of wine. A profound silence followed, in which she could hear the ticking of a distant clock that wasn't even in his apartment. He had a black digital model with glowing turquoise numerals. She fastened her eyes on 6:45, watching it turn to 6:46 and then 6:47.

"Everything," he said at last.

Dee looked over at him, startled. "Huh?"

"I like everything about you and I really want to kiss you. But I have a feeling that you want me to go slow." He gazed up at the ceiling, lolling his head back on the cushion. "All that stuff you said, you know, about your dedication to your work and how busy you are—I understand. I respect that."

Dee didn't remember saying any of that, not in so many words, anyway. Basically, she remembered how big the moon had been, and how good the takeout food had tasted in the fresh air, and how nice it had been to sit across from him at a very small table and talk about life. And flirt. Another sip went down, a larger one. "Please repeat the second half of the first sentence," she said carefully.

Tom sat up, and leaned forward a little, clasping his big hands together, his elbows resting on his thighs. He glanced over at her, then looked down at the carpet. "I really want to kiss you."

"That's what I thought you said," Dee replied, breathing a little unevenly.

"Would that be OK? Do we need a pre-kiss agreement or something, or would you be willing to just go for it?" He lifted his head and gave her a smile that was a potent mix of male charm and male uncertainty. Mingled with frank admiration.

Of her. Just as she was, in dragon slippers minus a few sequins and a baggy T, monoboobed, a bit pink in the face from the wine. The only answer to that question came immediately to mind. "Let's go for it."

"Woo hoo!" He clapped his hands once, a sound that echoed through the apartment. "Here I come. You ready?"

Dee swallowed nervously. "Yeah."

He got up, stood over her, and reached out a hand to pull her to her feet. She rose to meet him halfway, trying to keep her knees from wobbling when he got his arms around her and bent down some, so he wouldn't tower over her. The action pressed his muscular thighs against the lower half of her body— and she could feel his cock too. Fully erect. Down one leg of his jeans. His lips came down on hers, tentative and tender to a start. But Dee opened up like a tulip on speed.

Oh, yes. Could Tom Driscoll ever kiss. She was totally into this, encircled in a mighty hug, melting with sheer desire.

She slipped her arms around him and stroked his back while he kissed her, then slid her hands into his jeans pockets and got a grip on his butt. He grinned and broke the kiss.

"All right. Guess I can sweep you off your feet now."

He reached down and lifted her with ease, one arm under her knees and one arm cradling her back. Dee buried her face in his neck, loving the way his skin smelled—like the night air on the terrace, like the linen shirt he had on, and like—she planted little kisses under his ear while she thought about it—like a sexually aroused, hot man.

"Where are we going?" she murmured as he swung around.

"My lair."

"I thought you were living in the penthouse."

He carried her with ease into the bedroom. "I am. Sort of."

Dee tightened her arms around his neck, not wanting to let go, not ever. But she would have to. She ran one hand inside his shirt, brushing her fingertips over hard male nipples and the dusting of dark chest hair between them. Tom drew in his breath.

He set her down on the bed, not made but she didn't care. Dee leaned back in the tumbled pillows, her hair spilling every which way, looking up at him while he unbuttoned his shirt. He put his hands on his hips, letting the shirt front fall open while he gazed down at her, like he was taking in every detail of her, from head to toe. Then he yanked the shirt off and threw it in a corner, leaving his jeans on, and got over her on the bed, kissing her neck and ears, and then her mouth.

Dee sat up and pulled her T-shirt off. He pushed her gently back down, cupping her breasts through the bra, which barely held them. He pulled down the edge of the red velvet, making her nipples pop out.

"Beautiful," he murmured. She arched her back, and her breasts swelled over the cups. He took them into his big hands and got his mouth around a nipple, sucking for all he was worth, then did the same to the other one. Dee ran her fingers through his hair and watched him do it. His eyes closed and his lips tightened. The sensation made her pussy instantly hot.

Dee didn't want to move, didn't want him to stop—he was so into sucking and his caressing strength was turning her on. His breathing was ragged when he sat back on his thighs, looking down at her. His cock was fully erect and she reached out to unzip him but he wouldn't let her.

"Play with those big tits for me. I want to watch."

She made a move to unfasten the bra and then remembered that she'd fastened it with a safety pin.

"Leave it on." His voice was lower, almost rough.

She reached up to cup her breasts and gasped when he pushed her hands aside. "Never mind. I can't wait." He put his mouth over one nipple and squeezed both breasts, sucking hard on one, and then the other, moving up to kiss her neck and earlobe, sucking that next, moaning a little under his breath.

Tom seemed consumed by a rush of need that surprised her. He'd been so calm on the couch, even nonchalant. Now, looking down at her, bare to his eyes from the waist up, with the bra supporting her breasts from underneath, he couldn't seem to control himself. Reacting, Dee fumbled for his zipper and this time he helped her, holding onto the waistband and metal button so she could get it down quicker. He pushed his jeans down to just above his knees, boxers and all, and his cock jutted out.

Her eyes widened. He was huge. And thick. That thing was rarin' to go. He scrambled off the bed and got his jeans the rest of the way off, kicking them away before he turned around and yanked her sweatpants and underwear off with one swoop, making her ass bounce on the bed.

"Whoa!" she said breathlessly. "What about a—"

Tom pulled a foil packet out of the drawer in the nightstand. He ripped it open and sheathed himself with expert speed.

"Okay. That take care of that question—mmff—"

He shut her up with a kiss, getting over her on all fours and pushing her legs apart with his knee.

On a ragged breath, he reared back to look between her legs. Tom stroked her labia, then moved his gaze to her face, watching her reaction with an intensity that excited her even more. He touched her clit and Dee trembled. "Touch yourself there," he commanded.

"Then don't push my hands away."

In answer, he took her by the wrists and smoothed her hands down over her belly right where he wanted them. Over her pussy. She began to rub, almost shyly, then remembered doing just that alone in her bathroom, before he'd almost walked in.

"Say my name when you masturbate," he muttered. "And look at me. Don't close your eyes. I love that woman-in-heat look—drives me crazy."

She ran her fingers over her slick clit and whispered his name. He breathed harder and his sheathed cock looked like it was about to burst free. He grabbed it and pushed the rolled rim down as far it would go, an action that made his cock look even longer and thicker. Dee got two fingers at the opening of her pussy and played with her labia. He looked—and she thrust her fingers inside, moaning now.

Tom grabbed her wrist. He made her pull her fingers out and he licked them with sensual thoroughness. Then he put in his. One . . . then two . . . then three, just holding the fingers inside her, not too far but just right, while she contracted involuntarily around him. But she couldn't come. Not without a touch or pressure on her throbbing clit. He seemed to know that.

Tom pulled out his fingers and lowered himself over her, almost pouncing on her breasts, caressing them and tugging her nipples with sexy firmness. He reached underneath her with one hand, looking for the closure, and got the safety pin. In his thumb. "Ow!" he yelped, rolling off her and pulling out the opened pin. Then he sucked the blood off his finger.

"Sorry," she gasped. "I forgot I pinned it! The stitching's not very strong—you can just—oh!"

He bent his head down and took the side of the bra in his teeth, and jerked up. It ripped apart and he tossed it to one side, and jettisoned the pin at the same time. Dee's breasts were bouncing, and he buried his face in them, clasping one so that the nipple peaked and getting it into his mouth.

Tom stopped and took several deep breaths, watching her writhe beneath him. They were down to pure instinct now—no more holding back. He positioned himself between her spread legs and circled his fingers around the base of his cock, teasing her with just the tip.

"Please," she begged. "Give me it . . . all of it . . ."

Tom entered her with one fast thrust that made her cry out. For several intense minutes, he fucked her hard, plunging his aching cock into her tight, slick folds, turning into a wild man. He held her breasts protectively, lifting his body with only his strong belly muscles so he wouldn't crush them.

Dee kissed his straining neck, running her tongue over the cords that stood out, thinking for a second that he looked like a stallion, hot with sexual need and dangerously close to coming.

She knew without him saying so that he didn't want to, not before she did, and she ceased rocking under him, feeling him slow down and then still, breathing hard. A trickle of sweat ran down his temple and onto her cheek as he stopped to kiss her.

"I don't . . . I can't . . ." he moaned against her lips.

Dee realized that she was about five seconds away from coming herself. She slid her hands down his back and held his buttocks, pushing him into her with all her strength. Tom gave in, bucked, and rammed his cock in to the hilt, crying out and holding her in a powerful embrace that kept her from shuddering as she hit the same high. Once . . . then twice . . . and then he opened his eyes and looked into hers with a tenderness that shattered her heart.

"Oh, Dee," he said softly. "That was good. Much too good. Don't think I could ever get enough of that."

"Shh." She stroked his damp hair back away from his face and brushed her lips over his cheekbone. "Just hold me."

He rolled off without losing his grip on her. "You got it. You got me."

"So how come you like tits so much?"

Tom gave her shoulders a squeeze, laughing way down deep. "I know there are no stupid questions, but that one qualifies."

Dee patted his flat, muscular pecs, still damp with sweat from sex. "Is it because you don't have any?"

"Oh, geez. Is this a variation on that old penis envy theory? Hell, no, that's not the reason. Breasts are great. Soft. Smooth. Warm. Bouncy. I can't remember not being fascinated by them. I even ordered those X-ray specs from an ad in my big brother's old comic books when I was seven, hoping that I could see actual nipples."

"Boy genius." Dee traced her fingertips over his nipples, and he shuddered pleasurably.

"Okay, it was stupid but I was fascinated by women. Still am. The way they walk. Talk. Smell. Act weird and act wonderful in the same five seconds and never tell you why."

Dee giggled. "Trade secret. So what did you think nipples looked like?"

"Hey, I had to wait a few years. One of the bridesmaids at my cousin's wedding was wearing a strapless gown, and it came down when she danced. Wow. I was mesmerized."

"Then what happened?"

"My mom smacked me for looking. But once I got into high school, I began a serious investigation into the subject. Practiced hooking and unhooking for months on a bra I found in the laundry, so when the great day came—"

"Perv," Dee said indignantly.

"Hey, it didn't belong to my mom or anything. Some college friend of hers left it after a visit, and my mom washed it. But I swiped it before she could mail it back. She never knew."

"I see. But my safety pin threw you for a loop."

Tom shook his head. "You threw me for a loop, Dee. Totally naked, legs spread, playing with your breasts and pinching your nipples. Just what I imagined you doing when I saw you in that towel."

"Aha. Yeah, you did seem a little flustered." She decided not to tell Tom that she'd been having a great old time just thinking about him before he'd showed up. "Too bad Blastovik was there."

Tom thought back to the rest of his fantasy concerning his luscious upstairs neighbor. "I'm actually glad that damn bathroom ceiling came down. We might never have met."

"Speaking of bathrooms, I have to pee." She rolled away. "Does it still look like a bomb zone in there?" Dee sat up and bounced out of the bed.

"Nope. Just go under the scaffolding. Everything still works."

When she came back, he was lying there like a dead man, his eyes closed. Faking it? There was only one way to find out.

Dee admired him for several seconds first, sprawled and comfortable, soft penis nestled over big balls, and his muscular legs spread wide open. She walked to the end of the bed and kneeled between his ankles. He stirred a little when she started stroking him, caressing his calves and thighs, and he opened his eyes halfway when she slid her fingers into his pubic curls, massaging his groin.

His cock thickened. "Mmm," he said.

Dee moved up higher, pushing his thighs farther apart and running her fingertips over the silky, hairless skin on the inside of each. He relaxed, letting his legs fall completely open. She could see his cock rising but she didn't touch that. Not yet.

"Gets me hot when you just look at me. It's like I can feel you taking in everything I've got to give."

She smiled. "You know I will." Dee got above him on all fours, pushing his legs together with one knee, and letting her breasts brush his chest as she pinned his arms with her hands. No way was she strong enough to keep him still, but he looked like he loved being teased like that.

He gave a satisfied growl. "Unh. Oh, yeah. You can see what does to me." She looked down to where she straddled him. His cock shot straight up and twitched. "Put them in my mouth, Dee. Let me suck but not touch."

She scooted up a little higher, still pinning his arms, and let her breasts touch his face, brushing the nipples over his lips but pulling back before his lips could capture one.

"Not fair," he murmured.

"Tough luck." Dee did it again and he struggled to raise his head to kiss the soft flesh that swayed above him. Then he touched the tip of his tongue to a nipple, licking the tip eagerly. Dee let him, then moved to allow him to lick the other one. The sensation, in the absence of other contact, was subtle but very intense.

"Mmm," he said softly. "As torture goes, this is great. All I can touch you with is my tongue. And all I can see is the most beautiful bare breasts on earth. Your soft skin on my face—oh, God, Dee. Come down a little lower. Just let me feel that. Both breasts. Keep me there."

She obliged, enjoying this gentle role reversal, with Tom willing to be submissive, wanting her to tempt him, make him hungry for another taste of her nipples. Dee could sense her pussy throb, stimulated to an extraordinary degree because the contact was so restrained. The slight stubble on his cheeks was delicately scratchy against her skin, and that only added to an excitement that welled up deep within her.

"Tell you what," he murmured. "This next one's going to be just for you. Turn around and put your pussy over my face. Or lie down. Either way, be my sex queen. I want to eat you out like you've never been eaten out before."

Dee wasn't inclined to argue. She tried him out both ways, and when she was getting close, lay back. He kneeled between her legs, his erection high and proud. She reached out to stroke him and he paused to enjoy that. But not for long. "I'm saving that for later."

She raised her hands. "All right. If you insist."

He kneeled lower and applied his mouth to her pussy, licking very lightly. She got her fingers in his hair, loving that she could hold his head between her legs, and be serviced by a lusty guy who only wanted to please her.

Tom's lips enfolded her clit and he began to suck it just the way he sucked her nipples. Dee felt herself contract inside, felt a wave of deep sensation build and crest . . . and then she stopped thinking. He brought her to orgasm with stealthy skill, slipping his hands under her ass to squeeze her cheeks with each pulse of pleasure and didn't stop until she made him stop.

"That was even better," he said with wicked satisfaction. He wiped his mouth, then came up to cradle her by his side. And then they slept. The blue light of the setting moon woke them up about an hour later. Him, anyway. Tom got up to pee, then came back to the rumpled bed and stroked Dee's back until she returned to something like consciousness. "Talk to me," he said softly.

"You must be kidding." She favored him with a huge yawn.

"No, we have to talk. Otherwise you'll be on the phone to one of your girlfriends tomorrow saying that I didn't even talk to you afterwards, and she'll say I'm no good. I've been around the block long enough to know that's going to happen. But you can't tell them anything I say, of course."

Dee giggled. "Oh, there are rules? I so do not love rules, especially at two in the morning."

"Three." He waved at the clock.

"I hate you. I'm really not all that awake."

"But I am."

She yawned again.

"Ask me a question," Tom said, looking disgustingly alert. He ran a hand over her ass. "Or else I'll have to do you again."

"What a threat." Tom wrestled with her playfully, pinning her and kissing her until she was breathless and awake. "Okay, okay! Um—so what was the best pair of tits in your life?"

He groaned. "Fishing for compliments? Yours, of course."

Dee shook her head as well as she could, considering she was snuggled in his armpit. "I wanna know."

Tom fell silent. "Well, you really do have the best pair. But there was one . . ."

"One woman? God, I hope so."

"Yeah. One woman, but she happened to have one breast."

Dee managed to rise up on her elbow and look at him. "For real?"

Tom nodded, not really meeting her eyes. "She was older

than me, but not by all that much—she was a financial analyst at the brokerage. Anyway, she'd had breast cancer young and hadn't opted for reconstructive surgery. I didn't know that—I mean, she wore one of those things in her bra, looked fine to me. Hell, I was working so many hours on the trading floor I was just really happy to have someone to talk to by ten at night.

"She was different, didn't put the pressure on, didn't act like I was this rich guy she had to nail. Because I wasn't. Just a god-damn wet-behind-the-ears junior broker making about seven hundred a week after taxes. Anyway, one thing led to another, and she told me that she was really attracted to me but she was scared to death."

Dee didn't ask questions, just let him talk. The relationship had obviously meant something to him, judging by the quiet emotion in his voice.

"So I said something brilliant like, yeah, me too, and then she told me about the cancer. We had an affair—didn't last long. Her real guy had been in Hong Kong for a year working on a buyout, hadn't been all that supportive when she'd been sick. So she was, like, seeing if she was still sexy."

Was she? Dee wanted desperately to ask. Tom took a deep breath, as if what was coming wasn't all that easy for him to say.

"I really liked her. And she sure as hell was sexy—totally. But it took me about a little while to get over the way her chest looked, even though the scar was nice and smooth. And after that, it didn't matter. I did my best with the one . . . and it was a nice one. She found out what she needed to know, we had a fantastic four weeks of hot, crazy sex, and then Mr. Real showed up, and we went our separate ways."

Dee was silent. *My kind of guy*, she thought. *Totally my kind of guy.* She settled down next to him and listened to that big heart beat inside his chest.

"Do you mind that I told you that?" he said after a while.

"No," she whispered. "Not at all."

"And after her came the love of my life, only she wasn't and it didn't work out. I won't bore you with that story."

"Okay." Dee reached down for a blanket and dragged it up over them, kicking at the sheet to get it over their feet.

Tom turned on his side to give her a long, lingering kiss. "And then came you. I think I'm a pretty lucky guy."

She kissed him back. And five minutes later they started all over again.

3

Three weeks later . . .

Dee hung over the side of Tom's bed, looking for the remote. She felt around, not finding it. "Hey, no dust bunnies. You get another gold star."

"No remote? Keep looking."

"It's a jungle down here," she said indignantly, still hanging over the edge of the bed, head down. "Even if there aren't any dust bunnies."

"Have you been vacuuming?"

"Tom . . . I don't vacuum other people's apartments. Life is short."

"I wouldn't let you anyway. You have a very important mission in life: designing the world's most fantastic bra. Then you're going to model it. Drive me insane with lust. "

Dee popped back up and wriggled back to him. "That's not hard to do. You took the first one apart with your teeth."

He folded his arms behind his head and grinned. "One of the high points of my life."

Dee punched his side, not too hard.

"Oof!"

"You don't just love me for my tits, right?"

"No," he said solemnly, "you have a brilliant mind and genuine talent. And many other fine qualities. Probably too many for me to list."

Dee smirked. "That's right."

"Hey, my turn for some admiration. I have a cool career too," Tom said.

She went over the side again and resumed her search. "Yes, big man. You sure have a lot of socks under here. And what is it that you do?"

"The Driscoll Group helps money make money. Then my clients make money."

"If you pick the right stocks, isn't that sort of automatic?" Her question echoed beneath the bed. "Like when you leave two coat hangers in an empty closet and the next day you have twenty?"

"God, I wish it were that easy," Tom laughed. "Hey, did I tell you today that I loved you?"

"Ten times. I keep pinching myself. Hot sex and true love, not necessarily in that order. Is this going to last?"

"I hope so," Tom said easily. "But we may need more than one remote. On the other hand, I like the view of your butt. Keep looking."

Dee pushed away the strong hand that seized the opportunity to fondle her bare ass. She felt around some more under the socks, and pulled out a DVD case. Then another. Finally she found the remote, which she handed to Tom. But she hung onto the DVDs, looking at the covers.

"Oops." To his credit, he looked a little chagrined.

Dee laughed. "My, my. *Nurse Nancy*. And *Pussy Parade*."

"Classics."

She shook her head. "Still stashing porn under the bed? How old are you?"

Tom shrugged. "I'm a guy. What do you expect?"

Dee didn't really want to argue the point. "So what are these all about?"

He clasped his hands behind his head, and settled back. "Girl on girl action, mostly. And they all have big, beautiful tits."

"What you like."

"What I love." He curled an arm around her.

Dee nestled into his side, waving *Nurse Nancy* under his nose. "Let's watch it."

"Are you kidding?"

"No. I want to see what turns you on. I don't like porn because the men are usually gross and/or just too gay, but what the hell. Girl on girl doesn't bother me."

Tom brought her closer to him, laughing in a disbelieving way. "My favorite fantasy. Girl on girl, plus girl on Tom. Doesn't get better than that."

She pushed playfully at him. "I'm not saying I'm going to like it. I just said I'd watch it."

He snatched the case from her hand. "Okay. You're on."

Dee rolled back in the pillows as he got up, heading for the flat screen TV and popping the DVD out of the black vinyl case. He squatted to slide the DVD into the player, giving her a hot peek at his tight balls, just visible between his muscular thighs.

She indulged in a brief fantasy of telling him to stay there and watch Nurse Nancy and her distinguished colleagues get it on while Dee caressed him from behind, reaching up to stroke his lengthening cock. But he stood up too quickly and bounded back to the bed, cueing up the menu and pressing play.

A teaser scene flashed onto the screen. Nancy, a bosomy

brunette, was leaning over a male patient who was naked except for a sheet, which was already tenting. A very good-looking guy, Dee noted, who hadn't been waxed to store-mannequin smoothness. No, he actually looked like a living, breathing, really well-hung man.

Nurse Nancy seemed impressed. The actor reached up to unbutton her tight white uniform and her dark-nippled, firm breasts popped out. He stroked them and buried his face in them until the opening credits.

"I thought you said this was girl on girl," Dee said with soft surprise.

Tom chuckled and pressed stop. "It mostly is. But they threw in a couple of guys. I sorta forgot about that part. Do you like him?"

"Yeah. I'd even say he was cute."

"Want to watch?" He zoomed in closer on a freeze frame of the actor's mouth over the nurse's nipple, sucking hard.

"Okay."

She relaxed against him while he fast-forwarded through the opening shots, all of Nancy, bending over her patients and providing cheeky peeks of her bare ass and rounded, shapely thighs for the viewers.

"Mm-hm. Never mind skinny women. She's just right. Like you," Tom said.

"Go, Nurse Nancy. How come she never does anything but plump up their pillows?"

"She does more than that. Just you wait." He mimicked an actressy voice. "'Hello. I'm not a nurse but I play one in porn movies.' Don't you love the way she always has an excuse to bend over when she leaves the room?"

Dee watched the actor she'd seen in the opening credits throw down a magazine for Nancy to pick up. The camera zoomed in on her shaved pussy, squeezed between her thighs, just barely covered by the sheer, moistened white nylon of a tiny thong.

"Ready to eat," Tom murmured. He looked down at her. "You okay with this?"

Dee clasped his already stiff cock and stroked it gently. "Yeah. Let's see how it goes. But if Ron Jeremy shows up, turn it off."

He laughed good and loud. "Absolutely."

Dee looked back at the TV screen. Nurse Nancy just couldn't seem to pick up the magazine. She stayed bent over, her legs wide apart, as her male patient feasted his eyes on the sight of her shapely ass bursting out of her short uniform. The sheer white nylon over her juicy pubes didn't conceal much and the thin strap that separated her ass cheeks only made them look more tempting.

The nurse straightened up, magazine in hand, and strolled back to the man lolling in the bed.

Tom pressed pause. "You still okay with this?"

"Um, yeah. I'm curious. What happens next?"

"Here goes." He clicked play again.

Nancy resumed her indolent walk. "Excuse me, sir. I believe this is your magazine."

"Yeah," the man said. "I dropped it so you would bend over. You must like having men look at you."

"Uh-huh." The nurse favored him with a cool but lascivious smile. "I really enjoy sex."

Dee snorted. "No kidding."

The man in the bed pulled on his cock with long, tight strokes. "Do you like to watch?"

"Oh, yes. And you're so big." Nancy grabbed her patient's cock and got to work with professional speed.

Dee could feel Tom grin. "Great bedside manner." He gave her a hug and pointed the remote at the TV. "Had enough, Dee? Say the word."

"Yeah, that'll do it for me," she answered.

"No problem." He clicked the remote one last time and tossed it aside. Nurse Nancy dwindled down to a small white dot as the screen went black.

Dee relaxed against Tom and slid her hand down between his legs, taking his silky, stiff cock in hand. She didn't feel weirded out by the porn. The actor had nice, strong hands, like Tom's, and as far as she could see, knew how to use them just as well. Watching him hold and nuzzle and suck the actress's full breasts had gotten Dee hot. Her mind might hold back but her body reacted. Dee put her thigh over Tom's and pressed her slick, swollen pussy against the muscular warmth of his thigh.

"Want to get on top?" he said softly. "I could really do your tits while you ride."

"Not yet," she said.

He turned on his side to kiss her, opening her mouth with his tongue and sliding it inside, and nipping her lower lip in a wet, sexy way. Dee responded, loving the pressure and the warmth of the big, very male body enfolding hers.

Tom ran a hand down her back, reaching her ass with long strokes and squeezing it gently. He thrust his heavy leg between hers, pinning her, while he kissed her hard and deep.

Dee broke it off, wanting to look up at him, loving that sensual smile of his.

He lifted up some and pressed his erection against her wet curls, sliding just a little over her clit with the lightest possible pressure. The effect was wildly arousing. If he didn't stop it, she'd come in a hurry.

"Mmm," she murmured. "We should slow things down."

He wrapped her up in a passionate hug. "Just so long as we don't stop. What's your pleasure? Tell me."

Dee whispered, "Let's watch some more."

"Huh? Are you kidding?"

"No. I want to see how hot you can get."

Tom rose up, bracing himself on his elbows, planting kisses

on her breasts and nipples. "You're seeing it. I'm hot. If I get any hotter, it's going to be condom time."

"So . . . stay totally outside of me. Put in another DVD and turn off the sound."

He laughed and buried his face in her neck, biting and kissing her there until she arched back and laughed too. "Are you crazy, Dee? Women don't watch porn."

"If it's gentle and really sensual . . . I would. I mean, I will."

He stroked her face and looked into her eyes. "Okay. If you say so."

"Let's try it. Find something really sexy."

He rolled over and found the remote in the tangled sheets, clicking silently through the scenes until he stopped on the one he wanted.

"How many times have you watched this?"

Tom shrugged. "Who knows? It's useful on a lonely night. And I went through too many of those before you showed up in my life. But I told you about all that. Okay—ready?"

Dee nodded. "Fire away."

He got her settled by his side, and both of them were propped in the pillows when Tom got the DVD going again. The nurse, now totally naked, began to ride the man in the bed. Her pussy slid luxuriously up and down his shaft but only halfway. Dee could see his huge cock throb inside the actress. Nice. Very nice. She looked down. Tom was throbbing too.

Dee held him lightly but firmly, stroking Tom just how he liked it—up, twist around the head, around and down. She watched the man in the movie buck wildly and moan, holding the woman's cheeks in his big hands, while he thrust deeply in, over and over. His balls were tight, one coming up against the side of his cock, until he shuddered and came like a wild man, something that couldn't be faked.

"Whoa," Dee said. "That was . . . truly hot. But she didn't come."

"You noticed. There's more. Now for the girl on girl. You still okay with this?"

"Yeah."

The scene ended and the screen went dark for a few seconds. Then two women reappeared with Nancy, in a meadow this time, totally naked.

"Now where are they?"

Tom shrugged. "I don't know. Not the gift shop."

The trio spread out a blanket and began to take turns kissing each other, playing with each other's breasts and fondling each other's pussies, their bodies glowing in the warm sun and their hair shining.

"Come on. This part is so pretty it's like a greeting card." He turned over and slid his hand between her legs. "And it's making you hot. Want to try something?"

"So long as I don't have to wear a nurse outfit."

He kissed her lips very thoroughly, giving her more nips between soft thrusts of his tongue, then pulled back. "Nothing like that. But I'm too close to coming. If I touch your beautiful tits, I'll explode."

"So what do you want to do?" she murmured. "Wait a minute. Kiss me like that again."

He did, brushing her hair back softly from her forehead and kissing her with passionate tenderness. "I want you to watch the scene where the one with the really big breasts gets her pussy tongue-fucked by her girlfriend. But I want to do the tongue-fucking. How does that sound?"

"Mmm," was all Dee said.

"Do you want to be on all fours with me licking you from behind? Or on your back?" Tom stroked her sides, blocking her view of the TV but it was clear enough from the soft moans and begging for more what the trio of women were up to.

"All fours," Dee whispered.

"You're going to like this," he whispered back, kissing her again.

His erect cock pressed against her side and she could feel the first drops, warm and wet, on her skin. He was right about not being far from coming. He rolled her over. "Assume the position," he said softly.

Dee got on all fours so she could watch the trio of women, and Tom moved behind her on the bed. She wasn't sure there was enough room for his long, powerful body but at the first touch of his tongue, she forgot all about that.

He'd timed it just right. Nancy was on all fours in the middle of the blanket while her girlfriends stroked her back and ass. Then one kneeled behind her to do the honors, just the way Tom was doing Dee.

He lapped her tenderly, thrusting his tongue inside, then stopped, rubbing his wet mouth against her bare bottom. Dee trembled and stopped, tense but highly aroused.

"It's just a fantasy, Dee. You get to go into it, give into it, and come out the other side."

"I know," she whispered. "But I don't do women."

Tom ran his fingertips over her sensitized skin. "That doesn't mean you can't enjoy watching it." He kissed her cheeks, pausing to put his tongue deep inside her again just when the scene on-screen heated up to fever pitch.

Then he stopped and moved to her breasts, cupping them in his hands, appreciating their sway and bounce. He played with her nipples expertly, tugging them and then rolling a blunt fingernail against the aerola of one, watching how it made Dee sigh with pleasure. The woman on all fours was getting her nipples done too, by the third woman, while the second stayed behind her, thrusting her tongue more deeply into a pussy so juicy it glistened in the sun.

Tom moved back around behind Dee, getting back into pussy

worship, licking her labia and pushing his tongue in and out of her juicy folds, just the way he kissed her mouth.

The combination of watching oral sex and having it done to her sent shuddering thrills through her. He kept his powerful, very masculine body from touching hers, allowing her to imagine that a woman lover was eating her pussy with lascivious skill. Dee was nearly delirious with pleasure. Tom matched his tongue action to the lesbian love scene that was playing out on the screen, knowing exactly what she was watching.

His hands gently stroked the backs of her thighs, making her tingle with excitement. She began to thrust back against his face, wanting his tongue deeper inside her, trying to get every bit of it, wild to have her clit stroked to climax. But Tom got up, kneeled behind her, rested his big hands on her ass and made her stop. Then he ripped open a condom he must have had ready to go and sheathed himself.

"You're not in charge now," he whispered. "Imagine being intimately penetrated by a beautiful, dominant woman who wants you to obey. She wants you to have an explosive orgasm so she can see you lose control."

"Ahhh," Dee moaned. She felt him push the head of his cock against her swollen labia and not go in any further.

"Watch them, Dee. Let the fantasy take over. It isn't real . . . but the pleasure is." The woman on the blanket put her head down submissively, reaching around with both hands and spreading her ass cheeks wide, showing her swollen labia, begging silently for what Dee could see she was going to get. The second woman put on a long, thick dildo with help from the third woman, who tightened the straps as much as she could, making the dildo rise high.

"I want you inside me," Dee whispered.

"Not yet." Tom waited until the woman with the strap-on had positioned herself behind the one on all fours.

Crying out silently, the woman on the blanket pushed herself back, eagerly taking the strap-on as the woman wearing it began to thrust it in. The third parted her buttocks for extra-deep penetration, and the trio began to really rock.

Tom grabbed Dee's hips and rammed his cock into her with swift, deep strokes that thrilled her. She rested one shoulder on the bed and reached back quickly between his thighs, feeling his tight, hard balls tremble under her fingertips. She touched him, and then her clit, in strokes slicked with her own moisture, coming when he did, crying out when he did . . . and turning to collapse with him, held in his strong arms at last.

4

Two weeks later . . .

"So how would you rate our sex life?" Tom asked.

"This is a guy question," Dee said. "Like how many inches is my thing, how fast does the car go, and how big are those boobs."

"Yes. So on a scale of one to ten—"

"Eleven."

He beamed at her. "Really?"

"Yes, really. I didn't know hedge fund managers had such fabulously dirty minds."

"Yeah, well, it's something to do when we're not making millions." He grinned with masculine pride.

"Pass the marmalade. I need to keep up my strength. Last night was amazing."

He looked at her thoughtfully. "You didn't like yesterday morning?"

"Oh, shut up and read the paper." She patted his stubbly cheek affectionately and dropped a spoonful of marmalade on the rest of her buttered bagel, casting a glance over the style section. She took a bite of bagel, noticing that it was stone cold. Good. She didn't need the carbs.

Tom looked in the wrong drawer for a napkin, still not sure where everything was. Dee smiled and pointed to the right one. They'd slept in Dee's apartment, just for a change of pace. She still needed breathing room and occasional days off, especially when the sex was staying wild and crazy.

Which Dee loved.

Which was the reason they were having breakfast at four in the afternoon.

Having fun rolling around with Tom all night made sleeping through the alarm a necessity now and then. When it had gone off at seven a.m., Dee had been pretty sure it was Friday; and she knew Jami never came in on Friday; and wouldn't call if Dee wasn't there. No, her assistant left desperate, dramatic-sounding takes of sudden illness and needy relatives on the business voice-mail every Thursday night. Dee was impressed by the sheer variety.

She squinted at the caller ID when the phone rang, not recognizing the number but reading the tag. Love-Lee-Lace. The first ten thousand red velvet bras had been shipped to stores and the first sales numbers must be in. Dee felt her stomach constrict as she picked up the phone. "Dee Skinner."

"Dee?" a familiar voice barked. "Stu here, from Love-Lee-Lace. We got the sales reports. That new bra of yours is—hold on, I gotta unwrap my samwish and look at the mayo. The new counterman is an ignoramus when it comes to mayo. Never enough."

Dee heard the crinkle of white deli paper and the sound of Stu chomping. She held the receiver away from her and waited until Stu barked at her again. "Dee? You there?"

"Yes, I am. You were going to tell me how the bra was selling."

"The numbers are flat. That's not a good word in bras."

"I know exactly what you mean," she said evenly. "So what happens next?"

"We're pulling them, Dee. Gonna dump the rest at a deep discount wherever we can. The ladies love the way the red velvet looks but it seems like the construction don't do nothing for the ta-tas."

"Okay. I hear you." She let Stu rattle on while she covered the mouthpiece and filled Tom in on the details.

"Now," Stu was saying, "if you want to bring us a new design with the uplift that smart shoppers demand, we would look at that. But we can't finance another prototype."

Dee didn't know which was more annoying, that he was chewing on a squishy sandwich while he talked to her or that he used a phrase like smart shoppers because he thought it was cool. "Look, Stu, I'm in the middle of breakfast. Can I get back to you?"

"It's four in the afternoon," the lingerie buyer said loudly. "I got a crisis on my hands and you're eating?"

"You are," she pointed out.

"Listen, sweetheart—"

"Good-bye, Stu." Dee hung up and looked mournfully at Tom. "The red velvet bra isn't selling. Guess the magic only worked for you."

He put down his paper. "Are you serious? That has to be the world's sexiest bra."

Dee chewed on the cold bagel just to make herself more miserable. "Obviously that has a lot to do with what's inside it. He said Love-Lee-Lace won't finance another production run."

"I will," Tom said firmly.

"Oh no. Business and pleasure do not mix. We all know that. I road-tested the first one on you and look what happened."

"I ate it."

"Oh, be serious for a second. I was so sure the bra was perfect, I didn't ask Love-Lee-Lace for anything besides the money to make it. No focus groups, no marketing tests, nothing. So my fabulous creation is headed for the dollar stores. A fate worse than death in the rag trade."

Tom listened carefully, nodding his head. "How much money did you lose?"

"None. Why?"

"Then you have a clear slate. Love-Lee-Lace took the hit, not you. Creative people have ups and downs, good days and bad days—"

"But I have a bad bra."

"There are no bad bras," Tom said.

She put the gnawed piece of bagel back on her plate. "You're just saying that because you love boobs and bras and . . ." Dee began to cry. A lot. Then she wiped her drippy nose on the cuff of her chenille bathrobe in one disgusting but really satisfying swipe.

"And I love you. We're going to get through this. I think what you need is a new manufacturer. And we may have to bring in a tech team—you know, engineers who can get the construction down to a science—"

She swallowed her tears. "I love it when you talk man, Tom. No—no, I don't. I hate it. You don't know what you're talking about. Bra making is a lot closer to art than science. Breasts are just too variable in size and shape—that's why I thought the stretch velvet would work—are you listening to me?"

Tom folded his paper. "I heard every word you said. You can't give up, Dee. Ask yourself the big question. W.W.U.I.D.?"

"Huh?"

"W.W.U.I.D. What would Uncle Is do?" Tom said with annoying patience. "Would he tell you to just give up? No way. He'd tell you to follow your dream."

"I get the feeling you're about to burst into song," Dee said sourly. "This is my life. Not a musical."

"Then don't let one bad thing stop you."

"Okay with you if I tap dance into the shower now?"

Tom looked at her curiously. "You just took a shower."

"I know. But it's a great place to cry. And don't you dare offer me any sympathy until I'm good and ready for it."

Tom got up when she did. "How about money? Will that do it for you?"

"What are you talking about?"

"You're running a business. You hit a bump and now you need cash to get over it. First things first. Your staff. You don't have one. Write a glowing recommendation for Tank Girl—"

"Her name is Jami and she's a nice kid," Dee said stubbornly.

"Okay, so she can get a real job, maybe join the army if she likes their boots so much—"

"You don't understand. She can't bring herself to swat a fly. Jami would never pick up a gun."

Tom sighed with exasperation. "Bear with me. You have to hire some capable people. That's just my advice. You don't have to listen to it."

"Good. I won't."

He looked at her with wide eyes, still a little puffy from sleep. His hair stuck out every which way, and he rubbed it, making it worse. "I do believe we're having our first argument."

"And it probably won't be the last," she muttered.

He unfolded the newspaper and flipped it back to a sharply angled crease in the middle, looking annoyingly like a husband. "Dee, it's not worth worrying about."

"And why is that, Tom?"

He was pretending to read an article, as far as she could tell. "Because it just doesn't matter all that much in the great scheme of things."

She pointed the chewed scrap of bagel at him like it was a

loaded gun. "It matters to me. I spend way too much rolling around with you, I know that. And look where it got me."

Tom shrugged. "New products flop all the time."

She gritted her teeth. "How can you be so casual about it?"

He gave up on reading and refolded the paper, badly. Which was unusual for him. Even though his apartment was man-messy, he always arranged his paper in suburban-commuter-origami sections.

"Look, I'm sorry about the bad news. Especially since I was planning to surprise you. I went shopping yesterday. Bought you a present."

Dee got up to pace the kitchen, tying her bathrobe sash tighter with a vicious jerk. "It must be a very small present."

"Look next to the cream cheese. Behind the jam. Under the salt shaker."

She saw it. "Aww. A greeting card. You shouldn't have."

"Actually, it's an invitation."

Dee threw up her hands. "I don't have time to party, Tom. The next three weeks are going to be a work blitz. If you think I'm cranky now, just wait until I start on yet another proto-type. And brace yourself for my epic battle to come with Stu, the Love-Lee-Lace man. It isn't going to be pretty."

Tom got up and intercepted her in midpace to put his arms around her. Dee struggled and pushed at his chest. "Homicidal woman crossing, didn't you see the sign? No hugs."

"Dee, Dee," he said soothingly. "I'm on your side."

She relaxed but only fractionally. He rubbed her back through the chenille and the baggy T-shirt underneath it. Dee hated to admit it, but what he was doing felt good. Really good.

"Stop it," she said anyway.

He picked up the envelope from the table. "Read it."

She took it out of his hand and slid the card out, not looking at the design on the front. "It's not Valentine's Day. And it's not my birthday. Is this one of those just-because-you're-special-I-spent-$2.25-at-the-drugstore cards?"

He kissed the tip of her nose, rocking her a little in his strong arms. "You're beautiful when you're surly. But no. I told you. It's an invitation."

"Oh, right." Dee opened it slowly and glanced at the brief message inside. *"Tom Driscoll requests the pleasure of Dee Skinner's company—"* She looked up. "Well, I think you've already had that. Six ways from Sunday. I gotta get back to reality."

"This is reality, Dee. I love you and I hope you love me. Read the car—the invitation."

She sighed and read it again. *"Tom Driscoll requests the pleasure of Dee Skinner's company for the rest of his life. Marry me, Dee?"* Dee stopped and gaped at him. "Huh?"

"You mean yes."

"I do?"

He hugged her to him. "Well, you can think about it."

"Wha—oh, geez. I'm wearing this awful robe and I just lost a big contract and my temper and said nasty things to you instead of Stu and—and—I'm not even wearing a bra—and you want me to marry you?"

He slid a hand underneath the lapel of her robe and snaked it up under the T-shirt, holding her bare breast. "I swear on everything holy."

"You're crazy."

"That makes two of us."

She kissed him, hard, and that was all the yes he needed.

Noelle Mack is a designer for a major California entertainment company, and the author of several erotic romance novels, including *Three* and *Red Velvet*. Her novella "Tiger, Tiger" appeared in *Sexy Beast*. Noelle lives in Los Angeles, California, where all the men are perfect.

Take a scorchingly sensual peek at SIN,
by Sharon Page.
Available now from Aphrodisia . . . .

Venetia could marry. At twenty-four, she was on the shelf by London standards, but if she were very fortunate, a widower might consider taking her on. There was one in Maidenswode who had offered—he was fifty, fat, had eight children, and drank.

To return to the country would mean hiding her paints in the stables, sneaking out to the woods to draw . . .

She would have to paint in secret once more. After her mother had found that first portrait, of a nude male statue—painting had been forbidden. Her mother feared that it was the artistic temperament that made Rodesson so licentious. Olivia Hamilton had been horrified to discover her eldest daughter had been compelled to sketch naked men.

She stroked the ivory handle of her brush. What was he doing now, the roguish Lord Trent? Was he asleep, curled up with a woman or two in his bed? She could envision the threesome, with him sandwiched between, his groin pressed again a bottom just as it had pressed into hers, and the other woman would press her breasts and privates against his backside. His beautiful, sculpted backside—

The ache wasn't only in her quim—for some reason, her heart ached too.

If she were in his bed, in his arms, she could reach out and touch his bare back. Boldly trace the line of his spine down to his tight buttocks, to those iron-hard muscles she'd loved having beneath her palms.

What if she'd dared to explore more?

As though compelled, she bent and opened the lowest, deepest drawer of her desk. She should just shut it now. Instead, she lifted the first book from the stack. The rippled leather caressed her bare fingertips. Gently, she set it on the middle of the desk, so it wouldn't make a sound. Guilt made her heart pound.

In the middle of the book, she would find Rodesson's famed picture of a gentleman reviewing his harem of willing wantons at a Jermyn Street brothel. That gentleman, the Earl of Trent, was shown in aroused glory . . .

All she had to do was look.

All she had to do was open the book and satisfy her . . . curiosity.

No, that was . . . improper. Invasive. Rude. Unforgivable. But she could just peek. After all, the earl had performed in public. It was his own fault he had ended up in a book—

Really, one peek could hardly hurt.

She flicked past two courtesans entwined like the numbers six and nine to find *The Jermyn Street Harem*.

Trent was shown reclining on silken pillows, dressed in a dark blue robe, covered but for his spectacular cock which curved upward into the air. Dozens of women stood before him, displaying their breasts and quims. His lordship appeared as jaded as always as he selected one for his entertainment.

Throat dry, she studied the picture. Trembling, she traced his length with her finger.

This was so very wrong. To touch . . . him. This way. But she couldn't resist.

Was he exaggerated in the work? She doubted it. He'd felt enormous, impossibly so, when pushing against her backside.

His cock looked so rampant. Thick at the base, it curved toward his lean stomach like a sickle and was crowned with a large, dusky head. It was clearly the centerpiece of the picture, rendered in great detail—even to the veins on its shaft.

She found her fingers stroking between her thighs. The way she did, without conscious thought, while she drew.

Women were not supposed to touch themselves there. Even bathing was to be done with a cloth and with haste. But if she didn't touch herself, she'd die from the pain.

Rubbing in a slow, sensual spiral, she remembered his words. *"Do you touch yourself like this, sweeting? Do you paint your quim with your brush until you are creamy and wet?"*

She lifted her brush from the water goblet, stroked it against the rim to smooth the bristles and squeeze the water out.

Do you prefer two cocks at your command, or another woman's juicy cunny?

She thought of him watching her, amused, intrigued, with his hand on his large cock.

She wanted him so, this man she couldn't have. He was an earl—one who frequented the wildest brothels, lavished fortunes on the most desirable mistresses—but in her fantasies, she could have him. He would be hers.

Yanking up her skirts, she listened. Her door was behind her, closed. From beyond it, nothing but quiet. Feeling illicit, she parted her thighs on her chair and touched the wet brush to her nether lips. She drew a line of water to the apex and dabbed there, teasing herself with the cool wet against her heat. The sable bristles, soft but slightly stiffened by use and washings, rasped her clitoris.

She could just imagine the look of approval on Trent's handsome face.

Sliding the brush down, she held it tight to her bud and

rubbed herself against it. Wanton. Wild. Not longer caring about a delicate performance.

Yes, yes, he was right. She *was* wet and sticky. Heat and honey.

Oh, yes. Oh!

She had to hold the edge of the desk as the climax roared through her. She shook with it, rocking the chair on the plank floor. Her fingers dug into the blotter; she dropped the brush to the floor.

She gave a weak, giddy giggle as she imagined Trent applauding—

She gasped at the quick rap on the door.

Mrs. Cobb. The doorknob rattled. Twisting in her seat, she saw it begin to turn. She'd forgotten to lock it!

The book fell into the drawer with a bang just as her housekeeper pushed open the door and peeped through the opening. Facing forward, Venetia prayed Mrs. Cobb didn't notice her hiked up skirts, prayed that her racing heart didn't explode.

"This came in the post, mum."

Fluffing out her skirts as casually as she could, Venetia felt the hem swish over her ankles. She dropped a cloth over her painting in progress—it didn't matter if it smeared.

She knew her face must be beet-red but she had no choice but to walk over on shaky legs and take the letter. As she took it, she gagged.

"Pooh, scent! It stinks of the stuff." She sneezed. Her eyes watered. She stretched her arm out straight to keep the offensive thing away. Eyed it warily. Who would send a letter drenched in perfume? The return address was Compton Street, on the fringes of Mayfair. Instinct warned that this wasn't the sort of letter she could allow anyone else to see.

"Thank you, Mrs. Cobb." She began to swing the door shut.

"Is it trouble, mum?"

"No." She closed the door firmly. Guilt stabbed. Mrs. Cobb might like gossip, but she was truly concerned.

Venetia strode back to her desk and tore open the envelope with the end of her paintbrush.

Her gaze riveted to one word in fussy, lavish handwriting. *Rodesson.* She scanned the rest. *Your father revealed . . . can no longer paint . . . his talented daughter . . .*

Her stomach tightened. Nausea roiled in her belly. She reached the last line. *One thousand pounds to preserve your secret.*

Here's a sizzling advance look
at Jami Alden's DELICIOUS,
coming soon from Aphrodisia . . .

Suddenly a large, proprietary hand slid around Kit's hip to flatten across her stomach. She didn't even have to turn around to know it was Jake. Even in the crowded dance club, she could pick up his scent, soapy clean with a hint of his own special musk. Without a word he pulled her back against him. The rigid length of his erection grinding rhythmically against her ass let her know her dance floor antics had been effective.

What she hadn't counted on was her own swift response. Sure, he'd gotten the best of her in the wine cellar, but she'd written it off as a result of not having had sex since her last "friend with benefits" had done the unthinkable and actually wanted an exclusive relationship. She'd had to cut all ties and hadn't found a suitable replacement in the last six months.

Tonight, she'd only meant to tease and torment Jake, give him a taste of what he wanted but couldn't have. Now she wasn't so sure he'd be able to stick with that game plan. The memory of her gut wrenching orgasm pulsed through her, her nerve endings dancing along her skin with no more than his hand caressing her stomach and his cock grinding against her rear. His broad palm slid up until his long fingers brushed the undersides of her breasts, barely covered by the thin silk of her top.

She was vaguely aware of Sabrina raising a knowing eyebrow as she moved over to dance with one of the other groomsmen.

Without thinking she raised one arm, hooking it around his neck as she pressed back against the hard wall of his chest. Hot breath caressed her neck before his teeth latched gently on her earlobe. The throbbing beat of the music echoed between her legs, and she knew she wouldn't be able to hold him off, not when he was so good at noticing and exploiting her weakness.

"Let's go," he whispered gruffly, taking her hand and tugging her towards the edge of the floor.

She wasn't *that* easy. "What makes you thing I want to go anywhere with you?" she replied, breaking his hold and shimmying away.

A mocking smile curved his full, sensuous mouth. "Wasn't that what your little show was all about? Driving me crazy until I take you home and prove to you exactly how good it could be between us?" To emphasize his point, he shoved his thigh between hers until the firm muscles pressed deliciously against her already wet sex. "What happened earlier was just a taste, Kit. Don't lie and tell me you don't want the whole feast."

She moaned as his mouth pressed hot and wet against her throat, wishing she had it in her to be a vindictive tease and leave him unsatisfied, aching for her body.

But her body wouldn't let her play games, and she was too smart to pass up an opportunity for what she instinctively knew would be the best sex of her life. Jake was right. She wanted him. Wanted to feel his hands and mouth all over her bare skin. Wanted to see if his cock was as long and thick and hard as she remembered. Wanted to see if he'd finally learned how to use it.

And why not? She was a practical, modern woman who believed in casual sex as long as her pleasure was assured and no strings were attached. What could be more string free than a hot vacation fling with a guy who lived on the opposite side of the country? And this time she'd have the satisfaction of leaving *him* without so much as a goodbye.

Decision made, she grabbed his hand and led him towards the door. "Let's hope you haven't oversold yourself, cowboy."

"Baby, I'm gonna give you the ride of your life."

Outside, downtown Cabo San Lucas rang with the sounds of traffic and boisterous tourists. Jake hustled her into a taxi van's back row and in rapid Spanish he gave the driver the villa's address and negotiated a rate.

Hidden by several rows of seats, Kit had no modesty when he pulled her into his arms, capturing her mouth in a rough, lusty kiss. Opening wide, she sucked him hard, sliding her tongue against his, exploring the hot moist recesses of his mouth. Her breath tightened in quick pants as he tugged her blouse aside and settled a hand over her bare breast, kneading, plumping the soft flesh before grazing his thumb over the rock hard tip.

Muffled sounds of pleasure stuck in her throat. She couldn't ever remember being so aroused, dying to feel his naked skin against her own, wanting to absorb every hard inch of him inside her. She unbuttoned his shirt with shaky hands, exploring the rippling muscles of his chest and abs. He was leaner now than he'd been at twenty-two, not as bulked up as he'd been when he played football for the UCLA. The sprinkling of dark hair had grown thicker as well, teasing and tickling her fingers, reminding her that the muscles that shifted and bulged under her hands belonged to a man, not a boy.

Speaking of which . . .

She nipped at his bottom lip and slid her hand lower, over his fly until her palm pressed flat against a rock hard column of flesh. The taxi took a sharp curve, sending them sliding across the bench seat until Kit lay halfway across Jake's chest. He took the opportunity to reach under her skirt and cup the bare cheeks of her ass, while she seized the chance to unzip his fly and reach greedily inside the waistband of his boxers.

Hot pulsing flesh filled her hand to overflowing. Her fingers closed around him, measuring him from root to tip and they exchanged soft groans in each others mouths. He was huge, long and so thick her fingers barely closed around him. It had hurt like a beast when he'd taken her virginity. But now she couldn't wait to feel his enormous cock sliding inside her stretching her walls, driving harder and deeper than any man ever had.

She traced her thumb over the ripe head, spreading the slippery beads of moisture forming at the tip. Her own sex wept in response. Unable to control herself, she reached down and pulled up her skirt, climbing fully onto his lap. She couldn't wait, her pussy aching for his invasion. God this was going to be good.

If anyone had told her twelve years ago that someday she'd be having sex with Jake Donovan in a Mexican taxicab, she would have called that person insane.

Pulling her thong aside, she slid herself over him, teasing his cock with the hot kiss of her body, letting the bulbous head slip and slide along her drenched slit. She eased over him until she held the very tip of him inside . . .

The taxi jerked abruptly to a stop, and Kit dazedly realized they'd reached the villa. With quick, efficient motions Jake straightened her skirt and shifted her off him, then gingerly tucked his mammoth erection back into his pants. With one last, hard kiss he helped her down from the van and paid the driver as though he hadn't been millimeters away from ramming nine thick inches into her pussy in the back of the man's cab.

Kit waited impatiently by the door, pretending not to see the driver's leer. Like they were the first couple to engage in hot and heavy foreplay. Jake strode over, pinning her against the door as he reached for the knob and turned.

And turned again. He swore softly.

"What is it?" Kit was busy licking and nibbling her way down the strip of flesh exposed by Jake's still unbuttoned shirt. He tasted insanely good, salty and warm.

"I don't suppose you have a key?"

She groaned and leaned her head back against the door. "I didn't take one." There were only four keys to the villa, and when they went out they all made sure they had designated male and female keyholders. Unfortunately tonight, Kit wasn't one of them, and apparently, neither was Jake. "What time does the housekeeper leave?"

Jake looked at his watch. "Two hours ago."

He bent over and picked up the welcome mat, then inspected all the potted plants placed around the entry for a hidden key. Watching the way his ass muscles flexed against the soft khaki fabric of his slacks, Kit knew she was mere seconds away from pushing him down and having him right here on the slate tiled patio.

He straightened, running a frustrated hand through his thick dark hair. Eyes glittering with frustrated lust, he muttered, "There has to be a way in here."

"Through the back," Kit said. All they had to do was scale the wall that surrounded the villa. The house had several sets of sliding glass doors leading out to the huge patio and pool area. One of them was bound to be unlocked.

With a little grunting and shoving, Jake managed to boost Kit over the six foot wall before hoisting himself over. Holding hands and giggling like idiots, they ran across the patio. But Jake stopped her before she reached the first set of doors.

"Doesn't that look inviting?"

She turned to find him looking at the pool. Wisps of steam rose in curly tendrils off the surface. The patio lights were off,

202 / Jami Alden

the only illumination generated from the nearly full moon bouncing its silver light off the dark water. A smile curved her mouth and renewed heat pulsed low in her belly. "I could get into a little water play."

He pulled her to the side of the pool and quickly stripped off her top. Kit arched her back and moaned up to the sky as he paused to suck each nipple as it peaked in the cool night air. Her legs trembled at the hot, wet pull of his lips, her vagina fluttering and contracting as it arched for more direct attention.

His hands settled at the snap of her skirt. "I like this thing," he said as he slid the zipper inch by agonizing inch. "Kinda reminds me of those sexy little shorts you wore that first time—"

Her whole body tensed. She didn't want to think of that night right now, didn't want to think about the last time she let uncontrollable desire get the best of her. Her fingers pressed against his lips. "I'd rather not revisit unpleasant memories."

She caught the quick hint of a frown across his features but he hid it quickly as he slid her skirt and thong off, leaving them to pool around her feet.

"In that case," he said as his shirt slid off his massive shoulders, "I better get down on creating some new ones."

Damn, the woman knew how to hold a grudge. But the sting Jake felt at Kit's reminder just how unpleasant she found the memories of their first time quickly faded at the sight of her in the moonlight, fully nude except for her stiletto heeled sandals.

With her long legs and soft curves, sex radiated from her pores like a perfume, sending pulses of electricity straight to his groin. His cock was so hard he actually hurt.

In the clear moonlight he could make out the sculpted lines of her cheekbones, the dark sweep of lashes over her blue eyes, the full curve of her lips. Her dark hair swung forward over her shoulders, playing peekaboo with the tight, dark nipples.

His hands followed his gaze, tracing the taut, smooth plane

of her abdomen, coming to rest just above what he'd felt before but hadn't seen. Her pubic hair was a dark, neatly trimmed patch over plump, smooth lips. Her breath caught as he combed his fingertips through the silky tuft of hair, inching his way down but not touching the hot silky flesh that lay below.

He was afraid if he touched her he wouldn't be able to stop himself from pushing her onto a nearby lounge chair and shoving his cock as hard and high in her as he could possibly go. His hands trembled at the remembered feel of her soft pussy lips closing over him, stretching over the broad head of his penis as she straddled him in the cab. If the driver hadn't stopped, he knew he would have lost control, would have fucked her hard and fast until he exploded inside her, ruining his chances of proving he'd learned anything about self control in the past ten years.

So instead of dipping his fingers into the juicy folds of her sex, he knelt in front of her and removed her lethal looking sandals before shedding his slacks and underwear. Taking her hand, he led her into the pool.

He pulled her against him until her breasts nuzzled his chest like warm little peaches, reveling in the sensation of cool water and warm skin. He kissed her, tongue plunging rough and deep, just the way he wanted to drive inside her. He couldn't believe after all these years he was here with her again, touching her, tasting her. She tasted so good, like vodka and sin, her wet mouth open and eager under his. One taste and he regressed back to that horny twenty-two year old, shaking with lust and overwhelmed by the reality of touching the woman who had fueled his most carnal fantasies.

Greedily his hands roamed her skin, fingers sinking into giving flesh as he kneaded and caressed. He wished he had a lifetime to spend exploring every sweet inch of her. Kit gave as good as she got, her hands sliding cool and wet down his back, legs floating up to wrap around his waist. He threw his head back, clenching his jaw hard enough to crack a molar. Hot, slick flesh teased the length of his cock, plump lips spreading to cradle him as she rocked her hips and groaned. He backed her up against the smooth tiles that lined the sides of the pool. One thrust, and he could be inside her.

"No," he panted, "Not yet."

Water closed over his head as he sank to his knees, drowning out everything but the taste and feel of her. Eyes closed, he spread her pussy lips with his thumbs, nuzzling between her legs until he felt the tense bud of her clit against his face. Cool water and hot flesh filled his mouth as he pulled her clit between his lips, sucking and flicking until her hips twitched and he heard the muffled sounds of her moans distorted by the water. A loud buzz hummed in his ears, and occurred to him that he might pass out soon from lack of air.

Surfacing, he sucked in a deep breath and lifted her hips onto the tiled ledge. She drew her knees up, rested her heels on the edge to give him unimpeded access to her perfect pink cunt. He parted the smooth lips with his thumbs, lapped roughly at the hard knot of flesh, circling it with his tongue, sucking it hard between his lips as her pelvis rocked and bucked against his face. Every sigh, every moan, every guttural purr she uttered made his dick throb until he was so hard he feared he might burst out of his skin.

"Oh, God, oh, Jake," she moaned. Another rush of liquid heat bathed his tongue and he knew she was close. The first faint flutters of her orgasm gripped his fingers as he slid inside, clamping down harder as the full force of climax hit her.

Kit stared up at the bright night sky as the last pulses shuddered through her . Taking several deep, fortifying breaths she risked a look at Jake. His dark head was still between her thighs as he rained soft, soothing kisses on the smooth inner curves. Tender kisses. Loving kisses, even.

Oh, Christ, she might be in really big trouble.

She could never remember responding to a lover like she did to Jake. Then again, she'd never had a lover treat her like Jake did, either.

Her last partner was exactly the type she liked. She told him what she wanted and he listened, bringing her efficiently to satisfaction before finding his own.

But he hadn't looked at her like she was the most beautiful woman he'd ever seen. He hadn't urn his hands over her skin like he wanted to memorize every inch of her. He hadn't buried his head between her legs and licked and savored her pussy like it was the most succulent, exquisite fruit he'd ever tasted.

And he sure as hell had never made her come so hard that her vision blurred and her body felt like it was wracked by thousands of tiny electrical currents.

She heard the sound of water splashing, and her stomach muscles jerked as Jake held his dripping body over hers. Bracing himself with his hands, he came down over her and kissed her with the tenderness that almost made her want to cry.

Crap. What was wrong with her? This was Jake, the man who'd so rudely introduced her to the world of slam bam thank you ma'am. To give him credit he'd prove—twice now—that he could make her come. Really, really hard. But still. It was just an orgasm.

The smartest move would be to get up and leave before she fell victim to this weird hormonal anomaly. But her brain had ceded all control to the area between her legs that still throbbed and ached to feel all of Jake buried deep inside her.

And to think men got a bad rap for being controlled by their dicks.

She draped a lazy hand around his neck and slid her fingers into the wet silk of his hair. Then he was gone, water splashing as he levered himself out of the pool. She could barely summon

206 / Jami Alden

the energy to turn her head to watch him dig around the pockets of his pants.

Moonlight cast silvery shadows on the muscles of his back and shoulders, illuminating the drops of water cascading down his long strong legs. A renewed jolt of energy rushed through her as he turned, his cock jutting out in stark relief. Though she couldn't see his eyes, she could feel him watching her as he rolled on a condom with slow deliberation. Stroking himself, reminding her that in a few moments the whole of that outrageously hard length would be buried deep inside her.

She rolled to her knees as he waked toward her, reaching for him as he got close. He brushed her hands away, slipping back into the water and pulling her in with him. The cool tile was hard on her back as he pulled her close for a rough kiss. He lifted her leg over his hip, burrowing the tip of his erection against her. "I can't be gentle," he murmured. "I've waited too many years to have you again."

Hot nights mean hot fantasies . . .
don't miss NIGHT SPELL by Lucinda Betts,
coming soon from Aphrodisia . . .

Mﾐore brazenly than her waking self imagined possible, Iole gave her mouth to him, luxuriating in the velvet caress of his lips and tongue. His kiss tasted like something from heaven—sweet and powerful.

But fear rode in on the waves of surrender.

Sensations she hadn't known existed flashed through her with a burning intensity that left her breathless. The glide of his lips over hers made her instantly aware of her breasts, her thighs.

Her thoughts roiled, charged like a summer storm. Power raced through her fingertips. Might coursed through her veins, immense and building.

Like lightning in the summer night sky, she could sense emotions hidden by darkness. Something—someone—lurked behind the shadows of this tempest. Never had she known that nipples could long for something, that the space between her thighs could feel so empty. He—whoever he was—caused this.

The electric shimmering gave way to something more permanent, more pervasive. Yes, her breasts wanted his touch, his tongue and lips, but the molten feeling between her thighs was becoming insistent. The storm was building, and she couldn't ignore it.

Iole could only yield. She could only give herself over to pleasure she'd never understood.

But even as she ceded to his touch, even as she expanded with it, Iole sensed an incredible presence—someone wanted her attention. Someone as mighty as an autumn storm over Mount Olympus.

A god then. Which god? She couldn't tell.

She opened her eyes, searching, wanting to see her lover's face. What did magic look like?

But in the disjointed manner of dreams, he melted away. A pair of doves replaced him. They soared across an oddly colored sky. Green clouds, a purple sky. Then her perspective shimmered, and for a breathtaking moment she became one of the doves.

The warm air under her wings gave her the sky's freedom. Leagues of forest and farmland passed under wing. The Aegean lay opened before her. With a powerful stroke she flew toward the open horizon . . .

The dream melted to another.

No more wings. Now she lay on a rich mattress of feathers, subject to his authoritative touch. Who was he? As his mouth traveled from her hip inexorably towards her breast, she shuddered. As if lit from within, golden highlights shone wildly in his coppery hair.

With preternatural clarity Iole knew the line along her midriff that his lips would follow, that his tongue would lick. He traced the path, claiming every bit as his. Every bit of her longed for his heat.

His lips passed her navel, and Iole shivered in delight. The area between her thighs burned like a sun. She belonged to him.

She belonged. To him. Like an aphrodisiac, the thought enflamed her—from her heart to her fingers.

But that wasn't right. She belonged to no one, not like this. A chaste maiden, she belonged to her father, to marry as he saw fit.

Iole struggled to sit—to run. But her dream lover stopped her, sliding his long, hard body against hers.

His touch stopped Iole mid-flight—his body fit perfectly. He belonged there. And her dream lover took advantage, slipping his hands over her breasts as lightly as a spring breeze over the Aegean. The broad power of his finely formed fingers let her revel in his strength. She'd be safe in his arms. No one could hurt her here. His strength gave her the freedom to let go, to savor the new sensations he offered.

His fingertips danced over her nipple, hardening it. Mouth watering, she swam in the delight. He pinched, sending waves of shock through her. Who'd known that pinching would be pleasurable? Iole rolled her head back, wanting him to caress more of her, to caress her harder.

But still she trembled, and not simply with desire. No man had ever touched her so. This was wrong. As his fingertips slid over her nipple, fear slid down her spine.

Still, breathless and weak with desire, she allowed him to ease her back into the bed, trap her balmy body. He licked her stomach then, and the moan that escaped her dreaming self surprised the still rational part of her mind. She sounded like a different girl, a different woman.

When he cupped her breast in his hand, thumb still toying with her nipple, her head began to spin, deliciously. She writhed, arching her back toward him. Was she too forward?

She should wake herself. She should run.

But his hot tongue flicked over the curve of her hip. She knew she wanted more.

And he gave more.

When he captured a hard nipple and languidly licked it, she could only whimper.

Iole watched light from some unknown source play over the coppery highlights in his hair as he bent over her. She wanted him in ways she couldn't have said, even awake. He'd fill an emptiness in her she didn't know existed until now. He'd feed this growing, expanding hunger.

Each kiss worked its way to her head like strong Athenian wine. Each kiss weakened her resolve, her need to escape.

"That's right," he said, when he took her earlobe between his teeth. And when he kissed that ticklish spot behind her ear, her defenses weakened further. "It's only a dream," he said, his voice deep and melodic. Hypnotic. "Fly with me."

Her dream self acquiesced. He was right. What harm could come from a dream?

She wound her arms around his neck, drawing him closer, inhaling his tangy scent. Iole could not resist his call. When his mouth envelope hers, she parted her lips, welcoming his tongue inside. She embraced his wet heat, his soft strength, with a feeling of safety and well-being. She belonged in his arms.

That gods gave gifts, she knew—and she wanted this one. Iole took his hand in hers, and after a moment's hesitation, slid between her legs. She'd never done such a thing! Exhilarated with her daring, she widened her thighs, pressed his hand hard against the swollen nub that cried for his attention, for relief.

And the exquisite pleasure that came! White sparks exploded. The eruption of Thera's volcano couldn't surpass the power of this feeling.

As she molded to his touch, she dreamed that he cried in desire.

But it was only a dream.

*   *   *

Drenched in sunlight, Iole woke. Her attendant still slept soundly, oblivious to morning's arrival. As Iole stood, she became aware of the strange slickness between her thighs. Had she dreamed about . . . a kiss? As she tried to remember, snippets of the dream fell away, leaving her with the sensation that something important fluttered just out of reach.

Something very important.